SOME THINGS ARE BETTER LEFT UNPLUGGED

by Vincent W. Sakowski

ERASERHEAD PRESS

THE ERASERHEAD COLLECTIVE

ISBN 0-9713572-2-6

Eraserhead Press
16455 E. Fairlynn Dr,
Fountain Hills, AZ 85268
email: ehpress@aol.com
website: www.eraserheadpress.cjb.net

ACKNOWLEDGEMENTS

I would like to thank the following people for their inspiration and/or contribution to this work, big or small:

Edna Alford
Hertzan Chimera
Robert Fripp, Peter Sinfield, and the many incarnations of *King Crimson*
Mark Polachic
Jon Saklofske
Arthur Slade
Stereolab
D. Harlan Wilson

I'm especially grateful to the following people:

Kevin L. Donihe – editor of *UNPLUGGED*, and my newfound friend.

Carlton Mellick III – my publisher, and another new friend – thanks for making me a part of this surrealist collective, for your artwork, for everything.

Robin Sakowski – my wife, who has helped and loved me throughout.

Chris Stroshein – an old friend – thanks for your invaluable work on the first two chapters, and without whom this book may have never really begun.

And to anyone whom I may have missed: thanks.

Vincent W. Sakowski
September 1, 2001

SOME THINGS ARE BETTER LEFT UNPLUGGED

Dusk. Liquid without the warmth. Shadows long – along a gravel road. Hints and whispers of life: in the distance; the hills; the horizon.

The man walks. Like his surroundings: undistinguished in his features and in his wardrobe. Skin and suit: rough and tanned; long coat whipping out behind. Hatless.

Small leather suitcase in hand: as worn as the soles of his shoes, as worn as his soul. Well, almost. Umbrella between the handles pointing the way.

He goes up a hill.

As he ascends: first sounds, then sight. Confirmation. Construction, or deconstruction in the valley below. Men, heavy machinery: humming, hammering, howling. Warning lights flashing. Barriers all around, but he passes *between*.

The man approaches.

The conversation and the work stop. All eyes on him. Curious. Uncertain. Unfriendly. With a small wave from the foreman, three close in on him. Without asking, they pat him down, find he is unarmed, and take his suitcase and umbrella.

He doesn't resist.

The foreman steps forward.

"Identification please."

The man smirks. "Yours or mine?"

The foreman doesn't. "We only wish to ensure your continued welfare."

His smile broadens nonetheless. He reaches into a vest pocket and pulls out what appears to be a pocket watch on a chain.

Silence and stillness are redefined.

Then, the foreman barely utters: "My apologies, sir."

The man simply nods while glancing down at the works' complex face and replaces it in its home. Nothing more is said.

A large X is scrawled across the surface of his suitcase with chalk and it's returned to him, along with his umbrella, both unopened. The foreman leads him past several more barriers to the edge of a large pit, where everyone had been focused before his arrival. Sentinel work lights surround the perimeter, but even they don't illuminate the depths to any great degree.

The foreman points towards the ladder.

"Have a safe journey, sir. Things are . . . uh, different . . . below."

The foreman watches the man's descent, surprised at the ease in which the man climbs down the ladder, despite his belongings. The darkness envelops him, but it does not penetrate.

As soon as the man touches bottom the ladder is pulled away, but he is unconcerned. Eyes adjusted, he sees the outline of an extremely long tunnel, twice his height in diameter. It is the only way to go.

So he does.

The man's feet sink into the earth, sucking him down, but he resists. His strength increases proportionately as the dim light increases. The tunnel widens and soon he is walking down an alleyway. Venerable, dilapidated brick buildings on both sides. Lights out but life heard. Doors open but not inviting. Garbage replaces the mud. It's about as easy to wade through, but its overwhelming stench is difficult to ignore. The sky is dull gray. Still. Dead.

He is not alone.

Against one of the buildings sits a young woman in an oversized, moth-ravaged coat, buttoned blouse, and pants, with a large canvas bag in her lap, and her skinny legs held close. She may have been pretty once, but now, she is covered with as much grime and decay as everything else. Long, blond, greasy strands of hair hang in front of her face. Her pale features are almost wasted away, but they still have a certain edge to them.

"Evening sir!" She calls. "Lovely isn't it . . . lovely, as always."

The man hears the insanity in her voice. It is confirmed after he approaches and gazes into her phlegmy, bloodshot eyes. Decides to play a hunch.

"Good evening. I was just wondering . . . You see, I'm new around here, and I was wondering if you knew where I could find a place to eat, get cleaned up – that kind of thing?"

She rolls her eyes and replies: "Well, I see you were told nothing about this place. And that certainly isn't *my* responsibility. No no no. It seems nobody takes the time to face their own responsibilities any more. No, not at all."

He pulls on the chain and glances at the face again while the woman watches, visibly shaken.

She rants: "You had best take care of that bit of metal! Yes sir, you must! Disaster to those who take their possessions for granted!"

The man pockets it and smiles kindly.

"Wise advice. Thank you."

She calms herself somewhat; satisfied he has taken heed. Returning his smile, the young woman holds out her canvas bag.

"Would you like to see my misfortune? I have it with me always – right here inside my sack."

Her laugh is cacophonous.

Accepting the invitation he looks into the bag, careful not to touch it or its contents. Inside are fragments of glass, wires, white and gray metal, as well as various components. He nods knowingly, then leans back as she brings the bag close to her chest once again.

"Very nice . . . very nice one of those alright."

Laughing hysterically, she cries: "Top of the line, sir! Oh yes! Top of the line!"

He remains undisturbed and reaches into another pocket. A hint of mint is in the air.

"Gum?"

The young woman is silent, so he offers again. Remaining ignorant, she begins to spin slowly on her haunches while humming deep in her throat. The man has a piece himself, then pockets the package and the wrapper. He turns to go but is stopped by her voice.

"The contents of this sack is what remains of my microwave, which possessed some rather convenient but also startling properties."

"I see."

Looking into her eyes he sees the microwave: brand new, bright white, shining, sitting on a shelf in a small store. In fact, all of the wooden shelves are empty except for this microwave. Attached is an indecipherable tag.

Stepping back, he sees the young woman enter the store. She is *very* attractive: with gentle curves, long, fair hair swept back, and unblemished, creamy skin. After a moment's hesitation, she picks up the microwave and takes it to the front counter. The young woman places it beside a rather obese tabby, which had been asleep until now.

Alert, but seemingly annoyed at the interruption, the black and white cat shifts its eyes between the young woman and the microwave, confirming she wishes to purchase it. The tabby mouths a few syllables, presumably a price. The young woman considers its offer, then nods, yet she hands nothing over. After scrawling a large, black check mark on the side of the microwave, the obese tabby smiles for the first time.

"Enjoy your purchase, Mistress."

The tabby raises its paw in salute, and she is out the door with the machine in her arms.

At home, she too is all smiles, seeing the electricity flowing through her new microwave. Sighing in satisfaction, she turns off the light and exits the kitchen. The young woman feels the tension build with her desire to operate the machine, but wishes to wait for that particular climax in the morning when it will be almost unbearable.

Soon asleep, she dreams of nothing except microwaves: the time flashing, flashing, but never the same time twice – not only seconds, minutes and hours, but days, years, and other divisions of time she had never even imagined. Always turning . . . never faster . . . never slower . . . excruciating in its consistency. Always the hum . . . broadcasting the waves of radiation sweating from its pores. Until finally, shockingly, the ever relieving "ping" sounds off, and the door swings open. Whatever it was, whatever it is, is done. But her solace is only temporary, as she is placed inside, while the door is eased shut behind her.

Darkness.

Throb of buttons.

"ping."

Illumination.

Rotation.

Screaming.

Awake.

Awake. She rushes downstairs to the kitchen and snaps on the light. All is as it was. Or so she would like to hope.

"Why are you doing this? *Why?* I gave you a home. You were so lonely there. You were the last. I saved you! And this is what you do to me?!"

The microwave remains unmoved.

The young woman continues to rant while the time flashes in bright blue, until she can take its silence no longer.

"I'll make you talk. Just wait and see!"

Ripping open a drawer, she grabs a handful of silverware and storms over to the microwave. She clicks open its door, shoves inside the silverware, then slams the door shut. Babbling incoherently, she presses MAXIMUM POWER, 10 MINUTES, and ON, then runs across the room to watch the results.

The light comes on inside and the cutlery begins to rotate, but not for very long. Flashes of silver erupt, and the microwave is soon smoking and whining, until it finally stops. The machine has shorted out the power and she is in darkness. The microwave's contents glimmer and sparks crackle while bitter smoke thickens the air.

"That's it?! No explosion?! No fireworks?! Hmph. Well, it'll have to do, I suppose. You're dead now at least."

Exhausted after her outburst she returns to bed, somewhat disappointed, but content she will be able to get a peaceful sleep.

She is wrong, of course.

This time around there is no politeness, no initial complacency. The microwaves come straight for her radiating gold and mercury, flowing through her, cooking her inside out. From one minute to the next: nightmare merry-go-rounds riding on the backs of chickens, pigs, cattle, soufflés and casseroles. Too much sauce, and not enough plastic wrap. And always: the rotation. Always: the humming. Burning. Feeding. Living. Never the heroic "ping." Never . . .

Wake up.

But she does. Miraculously.

Shaking. Covered in sweat and drool she descends, but then actually bypasses the kitchen for the basement: *for the axe*. Stepping back upstairs she calms herself, intent on her action. Then she lets the axe fly.

Days . . . weeks . . . many months later the young woman is still there, in her kitchen, skeletal and suffering from scurvy among a great many other ailments. The remnants of the microwave are before her, mostly in a pile, while she tries to piece a few others together with duct tape and super glue. Then, holding up two large fragments of glass from the rotating table, she slowly revolves on the floor, humming, then soon muttering to herself:

"No there isn't anything faster. It will just be a moment, my dear." She continues to spin, until finally she stops and lets out the almost orgasmic: "ping."

Now. Eyes locked on the man before her, she hums.

Then: "Do you have something that needs to be reheated? Or can I whip something up for you? It's really a marvelous machine."

"Top of the line." He remarks flatly.

"Yes it is! You must have seen the ads for it, as well."

" . . . must have . . ."

"Well then, I . . ." And she pauses, confused. Tilts her head. Listens. "I've told you all I know. For what's my responsibility – "

He steps back. "I should be on my way then."

"Alright." And she reverts to her rotation.

The man makes his way down the alley away from the tunnel. Soon he is at an intersection. Eyeing each direction carefully, he sees an unlit sign on a tall brownstone to his left stating that rooms are available. He heads that way. Before he reaches the entrance, a burly, but ragged doorman suddenly appears, dressed in a maroon suit and cap, with most of his brass buttons gone. Half a head taller, and seemingly twice as wide, the doorman looks down and inspects him, his face expressionless as he takes in the gold chain and the small suitcase with the white X on it. He opens one of the two doors, then gestures grandly and waits for the man to go inside the dimly lit lobby.

Smiles politely. "Enjoy your stay with us, sir."

As the man enters, he notices an old sign on the wall:

MICROWAVE ON THE PREMISES

"Just what I wanted to hear."

The door swings shut behind him and he realizes once again that he is not alone. Hesitating a moment, he takes out the gum wrapper and places the chewed piece inside. Tosses it in a nearby garbage can.

"Can I help you?" A voice purrs as the man steps further into the lobby.

Before the man on the counter is the obese tabby, all fifty pounds or more of it.

"Perhaps. I need a room."

The man crosses over to the cat.

"Do you always gaze so strangely upon hotel managers?"

"I've seen you – "

"Really? I don't believe so. You're new here, aren't you? We've never – "

"No, in dreams . . . memories . . . You deal in some rather interesting properties."

"Ahhhh! So it's you at last. I wasn't entirely certain when you first came in, but now . . . Yes! It's good to finally meet you face to face . . . Word had reached me, but . . . well, let's not get too far ahead of ourselves. Rudimentary business first. Would you still like a room?"

"Certainly."

"Do I dare ask you to sign?"

The man smirks, then knots the fingers in his right hand. Bones crack, and he drives his thumbnail into his palm. A crescent opens and a single drop of clear liquid lands on the small, engraved silver plate before him.

"The Presidential Suite it is then."

Reverently taking up the plate, the obese tabby places it inside the till. Meanwhile, the man sharply extends his fingers. The bones re-crack, then settle in. The man sighs almost imperceptibly.

"I don't suppose you would like someone to take your suitcase upstairs for you?"

"Certainly."

"*Really?* Uh . . . but of course."

The man can't lose his grin. "Really. Sometimes a suitcase is just a suitcase. Sometimes."

"It's what's inside that counts."

"Most assuredly, but please, take it . . . as a sign of trust, perhaps."

"Perhaps . . . The umbrella as well?"

The man draws in a deep breath through his nose and closes his eyes, contemplating briefly.

"Something in the air . . . but . . . yes. Please. I'll be fine."

The tabby taps the bell and the burly, but ragged doorman instantly appears.

"Please take these to the Presidential Suite, and don't worry, the tip is well taken care of."

With a nod, and the man's baggage in hand, the doorman evaporates.

"And my key, please."

"Ah, I almost forgot."

The tabby lifts a paw, then pushes over a mouse's skull. The man takes the skull and pockets it without a second glance.

"How much time do I have?"

The tabby tilts its head. "That's a rather loaded question, isn't it?"

"Well then, to keep things more neutral – how much time before The Fray?"

"The Carnival is always operating, as I'm sure you know. And as to The Fray, it is very soon. But first, milk shakes and catnip for all!"

Gesturing grandly, the obese tabby makes its way towards the coffee-shop. The man follows, stepping up beside the cat, taking everything in: the odors, the mildew, the dust and disrepair.

"That's very generous of you."

"Pshawh. Think nothing of it. Just because you're my Nemesis, that's no reason we can't get along. There's so much for us to discuss. For you to see. But first, I'd also like you to meet some friends of mine, one of whom will actually be in The Fray tonight."

The man raises an eyebrow. "You're allowing that?"

"His lot was drawn so he insists, even though he could back down if he wanted to, of course." Sighing. "I've raised him; groomed him; taught him all I can. He's a major Gronk, my Prime Enforcer, but like I said, he insists, and how can I say *no*, considering your involvement and what's at stake this time."

"True enough."

"And here we are . . ." The cat pauses, chagrined.

The coffee-shop is empty. No customers. No servers. However, the air is thick with acrid spices and cultured bacteria: half-empty stainless steel cups and bowls of catnip are scattered across a corner table.

"Well, doesn't this bite the green wiener? They've already left. I really must've lost track of the time. You don't happen to know what time it is, do you? I never carry a watch, and so much for my natural instincts tonight."

The obese tabby glances down at the spilled herbs and the drops of cow juice, reading them.

"We should be on our way then."

"But of course. This way."

Taking the lead, the obese tabby eases its way towards the back of the coffee-shop, and soon they are in the alley. From here, the tabby and the man work their way through a series of streets and narrow passages all much the same as the first alley the man had arrived in, with one exception: they are alone.

"Is everyone at The Carnival now?"

"Not quite, but it's extremely popular, especially tonight. Word has quickly spread of your arrival . . . Ah, but here we are."

Before them is a shop, much like all the others. On the filthy window is painted the name:

Ye Olde Wonkey Shoppe

"Shall we?"

"Certainly." The man replies, and he holds the door open for his host. Inside is a small display room, but the worn wooden shelves are all empty, except for a thick layer of dust. It is the store where the young woman purchased her microwave.

Noticing the man's slight hesitation, the obese tabby inquires:

"You recognize this place, don't you?"

"Yes. After I first arrived, I met a young woman with the remnants of her microwave."

"Ahhhh! *Her.* She is sweet, isn't she?"

" . . . You could say that."

"And special, *very* special. Knows her responsibilities. The Mistress was the last; so how could I resist but be the one to make the final sale. Ah! *Sweet indeed* . . . But we dally. This way, please."

The obese tabby leads the way into the back room. Dust and cobwebs cover all. Boxes of all sizes are stacked floor to ceiling, and the man casually taps on a few along the way . . .

Empty.

Empty.

Empty.

Weaving their way through the maze of cardboard, their feet crunch on Styrofoam packing popcorn and dry husks of long-dead insects. Eventually the boxes become tents. These tents are far from empty, and they are certainly not drab. Unlike the shops in the streets, the tents are filled with stock, salesman and customers. Products living, dead, and otherwise are offered all around for sale and trade. The air is as full of sounds and smells as the ground is with animals, people, and properties.

After passing through several rows of tents the man notices that, with a few exceptions, there are basically four kinds of shops. First, are high-end stores of jewelry, china and crystal that only a very select few can afford. All items are triple-locked and encased with inch thick glass. So naturally, everyone aspires to own these items despite the astronomical prices. One tent proudly bears the slogan:

FROM OUR VAULT TO YOURS

And in *very fine* print in the bottom right-hand corner of the sign, it states:

A 25% shipping and handling fee will be added to all orders.
Insurance extra.
Have your lawyer contact ours.

Other shops carry local art and instruments, with the artists and their family and friends pitching to everyone in range. In many cases, passers by are literally pulled inside. More than welcome to haggle, they aren't let go until they buy something, anything. Although it's impossible to browse as the shopkeepers constantly thrust items in their hands. Along with the shouting and shoving, drums are beaten, rattles are shaken, and strings are plucked, trying to coax the musically inept browsers in another way.

Fortunately, since he is with the obese tabby, few attempt to draw the man inside their tents, not wishing to face the cat's wrath. And the man has no complaints about that.

The most popular new items are carvings done on old bits of furniture, hand tools and utensils. Nothing electronic. No misfortune to be found in these places. Rather, faces and scenes from happier days acting as totems, or demons from one realm over – as the saying goes – are portrayed in childlike abandonment.

In a few places, food can be found, including all the old favorites: cotton candy spun from worn, flannel pajamas, yellow snow cones, and the always popular mystery meat on a stick, because "Everyone Loves a Barbecue." The majority of the tents, including the food stands, hold souvenirs of the usual sort: pictures and postcards, junk jewelry, mugs and toys, and T-shirts, T-shirts, T-shirts.

The man leans over to the tabby. "I'm a bit surprised at the banality of it all. Is there nothing more interesting?"

"There are a few better places, but remember, this is basically for the tourists, and they'll buy anything."

"They certainly do."

"If we had the time, we could follow another path. Find a few tents with more exotic and exclusive items. Or, there are even better shops from one realm over that I recommend . . . Another time, perhaps?"

"Perhaps."

As the two wind their way through the crowds, the man pinpoints one voice above the others. A dark, teenage girl just ahead of them sits on a high stool with her legs crossed, in a long and tattered flower pattern dress. She stares straight-ahead avoiding all eye contact; hands folded in her lap. Shouts out at the top of her voice:

"COMM ON IN! ISA DEEFFRONT KINDA STORE WITH A DEEFFRONT KINDA ATTITOOD! NO 'IYHA PRESHAH SALES TACTICS 'ERE! NO ONE DRAGGIN' YOU IN! JUS' COMM IN AN' SEE WHAT WE 'AVE TO OFFUR! DAT'S RIGHT – NEW STORE, NEW ATTITOOD!"

The man glances in her tent as they pass: she has nothing different than anyone else, of course, but he appreciates her approach. After a moment, she starts shouting again, repeating the same lines.

He pulls on his gold chain and consults the face of the works. Immediately around him, everyone is motionless, quiet, including the teenage girl, but only for a moment. Confirmation: *It's him. He's here!* The Word spreads. Seemingly satisfied, the man pockets the works and follows the obese tabby.

While twisting and turning past the tents they are interrupted by a garishly dressed old woman, in a patchwork skirt and a multitude of scarves tied all the way down the sleeves of her billowy blouse. Her round face is creased with wrinkles, and her black eyes focus on the man. She steps directly in front him, maneuvering herself between him and the obese tabby. The old woman reaches out to him with gnarled, arthritic fingers, charms tinkling on her wrists, but she doesn't quite make contact.

Immediately, the obese tabby signals to its henchmen hidden in the crowd, some of whom have stopped to watch this minor spectacle. Most people, however, pass by taking no heed, even though it involves the obese tabby, which is known by all.

Eyes wild but pleading, the old woman starts to drool. Her dirty hands remain stretched out towards the man. Fingers flexing. Chin glistening. Spittle hanging.

"Excuse me, sir: would you like me to tell you your misfortune? It only–"

"No. Thank you very much. If you'll excuse us, we're late."

"But please, sir – " She steps in closer, almost touching him, her breath ripe. Rancid. "I have things to tell you – "

Suddenly, five hairless, faceless Goons surround them. Grabbing her firmly in their gloved hands they take her away, muffling her cries. The man does not interfere, nor does anyone else around. Rather, everyone parts quickly before the Goons draw too close.

A short distance away, the misfortune teller bites through the gloved hand covering her mouth with the few teeth rotten she has left. She cries out to the man:

"All is not as it seems, sir! ALL IS NOT AS IT SEEMS!!!!!"

Her mouth is quickly covered again and no amount of biting will release the grip on her.

The obese tabby snickers. "Now tell us something we don't already know." But it stops when it sees that the man is not laughing as well.

The man looks down solemnly at the cat.

"Make sure she is not harmed."

" . . . But of course."

The obese tabby nods and signals to its henchmen. After another moment, the feline leads the way once more. The two make their way in silence as the people part before them.

Beyond The City of Silk and Canvas, there is an amusement park to one side and a stadium sunk deeply into the ground on the other. From the park, always the screaming, the screeching. Never solace. Never enough. It holds little attraction for the man right now, so he pays it no mind. But within the stadium: Three-Ring Circus. Ring One: trapeze – high in the air – performers sweating, swinging, singing, spinning. Below: no net. Only a massive pool of liquid mercury fills the ring.

Accompanying the performance, no calliope or brass but, three pale yet beautiful women with long, flowing hair, wearing ivory bodices, bloomers, hose, and hoop skirt frames bow cellos in a nearby corner. Long, heavy, sorrowful notes are drawn out in one verse, as the artists simply swing back and forth. In the next, as they begin to fly again, the strings are bowed and hammered, distorted through their amplifiers. Feedback ripples and chills the air. Enraptured, many people who were once weeping, now sit terrified, their hair bristling, their mouths agape. Waiting.

The man pauses, interested, the old woman a memory.

More than happy to see the man brightening again and wanting to capitalize on the moment, the tabby explains:

"They are the best, of course. So they rarely fall, but – "

As if on cue, one artist misses the crossbar and falls to the silvery sea below. There is a scream of strings and a cry from the crowd as she drops. Landing solidly, she causes a slight ripple and splash on the surface, but doesn't sink. Immediately, the music changes to a simple multiple bass line, sounding much like: "dumb-dumb-dumb-dumb . . . dumb-dumb-dumb-dumb," then: "doom-doom-doom-doom . . . doom-doom-doom-doom." It begins slowly, but gradually the tempo increases. The man sees the mercury absorbed into the petite artist's skin – which is barely covered by her skimpy, sequined costume – even as she rolls off the pool, unassisted. He sees the liquid death coursing through her lean body and the insanity building within her as she dizzily climbs up the ladder to take her place once again.

The audience is ecstatic.

The other artists continue swinging back and forth while the crowd grows frenzied, waiting for the one who fell to try again.

Having seen enough, the man shifts his gaze to the caged center ring, where a humanoid body of black and blue question marks stands with a whip in one of its "hands." Twelve figures sit poised and hungry inside the cage's perimeter. The man grins as he recognizes all the figures waiting angrily and anxiously. Included are: an ancient tome fanning its pages, a grandfather clock, a full-length silver mirror, a movie camera, a computer with its mouse held high and spinning, and a massive gold chain coiled like a snake, among the many others. Like the young woman's microwave, all have a black check mark on one side.

The man doesn't wait to see who makes whom leap through the fire, but glances over at Ring Three, which is overflowing with diminutive clowns. Or at least, they seem like clowns. Baggy clothes. Rainbow hair and make-up. Red, rubber noses and big, floppy shoes. But, he's never seen clowns wield flaming swords twice their size. At their feet wooden crates are stacked and scattered, filled with clear glass bottles, topped off with some gray metallic liquid. The crates are labeled:

BARBED BOTTLED CHAINS

Before the man makes any sense of what's happening there, however, the tabby ushers him along, saying:

"The Fray is about to begin."

They make their way through the throngs of people, which respectfully part for them as they see their approach. Among them are scores of hairless, faceless Goons, and also many others like the young woman that the man had first met: diseased and delirious, carrying around their misfortune – most of them ranting at anyone nearby. A few even possess relics like radio eyes and television shoes. Briefly, he searches for the young woman, having a greater understanding of the situation here – wanting to re-establish contact right now, despite his pull towards The Fray. But she is nowhere to be seen as he is ushered along.

Finally, they arrive at The Coliseum – which is less than standing room only – and they glide through to the arena floor. Once there, the mobs erupt. Although, thankfully, their apocalyptic cacophony doesn't quite reach them down there.

"Ah, here we are."

Cracking a grin, the obese tabby amiably waves at the Gronk standing on the other side of the shallow pool. The pool is roughly the size of a boxing ring, with clear glass walls one foot high, an inch thick, and its contents only a couple of inches deep. It has the purity of fresh spring water.

"Sorry to be late, my friend. I lost track of the time."

Remaining unmoved, the massive male steps towards the edge, and pauses there with his bulging, sinewy arms crossed. A brightly polished stainless steel skullcap is tightly bolted to his head, while a finely contoured bronze breastplate is hooked through the flesh of his torso. Only his nipples are exposed. Both his forearms and his thighs have thin bands of gold and silver woven through them both vertically and horizontally. Around his groin and on his feet up to his knees is a rough, beige skin of unfamiliar original.

The man lets out a low, appreciative whistle.

"Is he still in much pain?"

"Constantly. That's a large part of the reason he does all that. Yes. The pain never ends and he enjoys every moment of it. But as you see, for The Fray we have protected his feet and groin. Otherwise, there wouldn't be much of a battle with no feet to stand on, and well . . . I'm not sure if he'd miss his genitals or not, but it's in the rules."

Overhead, a crow squawks and welcomes the crowd:

"GOOOOOOOD EEEEEVENNINNNG LAAAAADIEEEEEESS ANNNNNNNNNND GENNNNTLLEMENNNNNNNNNN!!!!!!!! WELCOME TO THIS EVENING'S FRAY – THE BATTLE TO END ALL BATTLES!!!! That is, until we have another one! WHERE ARMAGEDDON IS NEVER AN END!!!! WHERE GOOD AND EVIL – "

An oceanic roar of laughter crashes over The Coliseum.

The crow squawks, snickering. Cackling.

"ALRIGHT‼ Alright! Just kidding folks! I see that we have a lively and most worthy audience this evening, which obviously knows what this is all about! LET ME HEAR YOU‼‼"

The masses erupt: "SHADES OF GRAY‼‼‼ SHADES OF GRAY‼‼‼ SHADES OF GRAY‼‼‼ SHADES OF GRAY‼‼‼"

The crow flaps its wings, calling for silence.

"And for you, my most worthy audience, we have the worthiest of opponents, and the greatest Prize to date for the victor!"

And the crow carries on for several minutes: giving the vital statistics of the two opponents, and setting the final odds for the betting.

"Are you ready?" The obese tabby inquires.

The man nods and takes a step back from the pool edge. He takes off his long coat and carefully places it on a nearby chair. Next, he removes his suit coat and tie. After undoing the top two buttons of his white shirt and rolling up his sleeves, he unbuttons his embroidered vest, but stops at the hole where the chain passes through. He unties the chain, then draws the works out and places it in his left hand.

The throngs begin to stomp and throw their arms in the air chanting:

"FRAY‼ FRAY‼‼ FRAY‼‼‼ FRAY‼‼‼ FRAY‼‼ FRAY‼‼ FRAY‼‼‼ FRAY‼‼‼"

With a gesture from the man the mob is silenced. The man knots his fingers in a different configuration this time, then clicks and grinds a few incomprehensible words over the works. It begins to hum and tremble in the man's hand, and he gently places it on a small platform at the edge of the pool, opposite to the obese tabby's Prime Enforcer. He unknots his fingers and steps back beside the cat. The two take their seats, which have been set out nearby on The Coliseum's floor.

The works grow, pulsing and bleating until it is half the size of the Gronk. Golden gears extend, spinning like saw blades. Numerous cables sparking with electricity slither their way out through various openings and act as both arms and legs. The works glow and whirls on its platform waiting for The Fray to begin.

The crow squawks overhead: "You both know the rules, but let me remind you that there is no intentional splashing, and only one of you can leave the pool. If you hear me squawk you must stop and move to a neutral corner until a ruling is made and I tell you to begin again. Understood? Good! NOW LET THE FRAY BEGIN‼‼‼"

The masses erupt once again, and this time they will not be silenced.

The Gronk and the works enter the pool and square off against one another, searching for an opening. Unfortunately for the works, it does not have the protective skin and the molecular acid is slowly eating at it. They circle one another for almost a minute before the Gronk finally lunges at the works and attempts to grapple with it. The works is extremely solid and heavy, even for the Gronk, and they are left pulling at each other without gaining any real advantage. Acid is kicked up repeatedly, however, and so the real Fray has begun.

The masses grow exponentially wilder as they see more and more flesh and metal being eaten away by the acid. Blood flows freely from multiple burns and cuts on the Gronk's body, while many of the works' inner mechanisms are exposed.

The man and the obese tabby sit by and watch in silence. Both are excited, yet deeply concerned, as they see The Fray do its work on their loved ones. There is no anger, no malice – only mutual respect, and a desire for a quick end to the Fray, either way.

Then, in a massive surge of strength, the Gronk picks up the works and prepares to slam it into the acid. As he draws it up, however, acid rains down on him – on his face, in his eyes, under all of his metal plating. Despite the excruciating pleasure he derives from the acid, it's more than his body is willing to endure. Thus, rather than casting the works down and out in victory, the works fall upon him. The great weight pins him to the acid pool, and the works muffle the rapturous cries of the Prime Enforcer as his life is burned and melted away. The air is putrid and metallic.

The crow squawks and the works is declared the winner. Immediately, the man is on his feet and waits at the edge for the works to come back to him. Meanwhile, the obese tabby remains seated, mewing forlornly to itself, as it watches its pet gradually dissolve.

The mobs are on the verge of revolution but are quickly contained. The winners are paid off and the losers know there will always be another Fray for them to possibly win their fortunes back. Besides, many realize that it is not simply about winning or losing but about being properly entertained that matters the most. Except for the loser of the Fray, of course – the only possible consolation is a quick death. Although, not this time around.

The works reach the edge of the pool, half-eaten, and whining sickly, but it's still alive. Barely. Before the man reaches for the works, however, a crew completely covered in suits made of the protective skin, moves expediently in front of him. They lift the works out of the pool, place it on the platform and generously spray it, washing the remaining acid away.

Their job complete, the crew promptly vacates the area. Stepping forward, the man grasps the works with both hands and recites a short but almost incomprehensible melody. Shuddering and groaning, the works begins to shrink back to its former size. All of its appendages retreat while the man takes it up carefully his hands. After it's finally finished, the man crunches his fingers for the third time that night and releases a single, clear drop over the works. The mechanism sighs in some relief, but it's still in critical condition. Cradling it lovingly, the man coos at it for some time.

Eventually the obese tabby waddles over to the man. It reaches out a paw, which the man shakes gently.

They stand together in silence for some time, until the cat finally utters:

"I really miss The Words."

The man nods. "Yes. Far less brutal. Much more tasteful than The Fray."

"Distinguished."

"Exactly."

"Powerful."

"Truly."

"Perhaps we can play another time."

"Certainly."

"And now I imagine you would like to collect The Prize."

The man sighs. Shakes his head. "I'm in no great hurry."

"No?"

"No. I'm not ready for it yet. Besides, as you said before The Fray began: there's so much to discuss; for me to see; and there's no reason why we can't get along, even though I'm your Nemesis."

A soft smile grows on the feline's face.

"You truly are a gentleman."

"Thank you. But perhaps we should move along. I'm in no mood for interviews, and there's much healing to be done."

"There certainly is at that."

Gazing around, the obese tabby takes in the pool one last time. It's still hissing and bubbling over the remnants of feline's Prime Enforcer. Sadly, its eyes move up along the crowds and into the sky.

"It looks like it may rain shortly. Perhaps you should've brought your umbrella."

Cradling the works in one hand, the man takes up his clothes with the other.

"Perhaps . . . Perhaps. But no matter now . . . Shall we?"

"But of course."

And with that, the two walk together, away from The Carnival, and away from all that is made to keep them at odds.

For the time being, anyway.

THIS NIGHT WOUNDS TIME

Afternoon. Early. Radiation reaching its zenith: eating at the stone and steel of the streets, of the sidewalk. All is immaculate. As always. Not a hint of waste or dilapidation.

The man walks – with purpose. His destination known, but only as a memory – and it's someone else's memory he's using right now. As he passes the various shops, he observes everything with a critical but not unfriendly eye.

In front of many of the shops clerks keep busy, hosing down the sidewalk; the facades; sweeping or painting. No one is still but all is silent, relatively speaking, of course. Inside each window the man sees the same thing, or rather the lack of it: none of the stores appear to have anything to sell. All of the shops are overstaffed and open for business, but all of the shelves are completely empty. People are cleaning, repairing fixtures, and generally appear to be preparing for customers, but again, there is nothing to be seen for sale. Yet, everyone seems to be quite happy in his or her vocation, and like the shops, everyone is immaculate.

Eventually the man reaches his destination. A bright green and magenta neon sign flashes in the window of a coffee-shop and proclaims:

EGO SIDEROAD'S
Open 24 Hours!

Taped to the window in the corner are two other finely drawn handmade signs:

Drive Thru is Being
Closed For Repairs.
Sorry. Mgmt.

And:

HELP WANTED!
Apply Within

As the man pushes on the door, a bell begins to ring and a chorus echoes through the coffee-shop.

"ALLELUIA!! ALLELUIA!!
AL-LEEEEEELUUIA!!"

The man barely raises an eyebrow. Casually, he crosses the room and sits on a stool at the main counter. He swivels on his seat just to confirm it's possible, then spins around several times, taking in the room. He tries to match the speed of the fans turning overhead, which isn't particularly difficult, but it's fun. Normally he would never even consider indulging himself in such a way publicly, but Ego's has resurrected the nostalgic bones in his body. However, he soon allows himself to slow until he finally stops, and he further enjoys the slight head rush he quickly receives as payment for his revolution. Overall, he is rather impressed.

The coffee-shop is intensely lit with sodium arc lights hanging on almost invisible lines from the ceiling, causing everything in the room to glow: chrome, steel, Formica, Mack-Tack with delusions of grandeur. Pictures of even better days than these crowd the walls, and the man is almost surprised how it's possible for the people to have larger smiles than they do now. Mauve, aqua, and ivory predominate the color scheme. Like every other shop the man has seen, Ego Sideroad's is spotless.

Only one booth is occupied: by a couple – a flamboyantly dressed old woman and a rather large snake, a constrictor. The man recognizes the old woman covered with ribbons and lace as the misfortune teller from The Carnival. But before the man can absorb their situation, a pretty young woman taps him on the shoulder from the other side of the counter. He makes the half spin his denouement and settles before her.

"Coffee?"

The man nods once, then watches as the waitress in a crisp peach dress prepares to serve him. From under the counter, with swift professional precision, she lays out cream, sugar, a spoon, and a cup and saucer. Everything gleams. The man sees his image distorted in countless ways and he can't help but chuckle at the sights before him.

Meanwhile, the young woman goes to the immense stainless steel coffee machine. It is the only appliance on the far counter and the only apparent source of sustenance in the whole establishment. With holy reverence, the waitress carefully pours out the steaming charcoal liquid, leaving a comfortable margin at the top of the cup. Not a drop is wasted and, maintaining her somber countenance, she replaces the coffeepot on its heating coils. With the pot safely at rest, the waitress turns back to the man and confirms that it is a job well done.

The man smiles his thanks and the young woman blushes. He continues to keep his eyes locked on the waitress, wanting to speak, but hesitant to do so for the moment. Finally, in a fit of nervousness, the waitress bursts out:

"Do I know you? Have we met before?"

"No. Not yet."

The waitress considers this. Then: "What about now?"

"Now is past. It always is this way."

"I see."

Chuckling. "You probably don't, but that's OK."

"Are you making fun of me? Because in our union – "

"No. Not at all. Please forgive me."

The waitress feels the weight of his apology; she is uncomfortable she made him do it.

"That's alright. There's nothing to forgive."

"You're very gracious."

"It's a part of my job." Her discomfort grows.

"No. It's a part of you."

Twisting her spotless apron in her hands. "Who are you? Do I know you? Why are you saying these things to me? Why are you here?"

"You are actually serving something – "

"Yes. I am the last."

"But really, I'm simple here to see you . . . to see what was . . . to get to know you somewhat . . . before – "

"Before what?"

"Simply *before* . . . before we meet again for the first time."

"Maybe you should just drink your coffee and leave me alone. Or maybe you should – "

"Wait." Leans back. Arms open. "Tell me: whom or what do you see sitting before you?"

"The obese tabby. What else am I supposed to be seeing?"

"Nothing . . . Nothing . . . My apologies once again." Grins. Leans in. Elbows on the counter. "I don't mean to be intrusive. Normally I – I'm simply feeling a little giddy, I suppose. I – "

"I really have a lot of work to do."

Before the man can say anything more, the young woman steps away and disappears underneath the counter. The man can hear her rummaging around, whispering to herself, but soon he lets her go. He realizes he is getting too caught up in the moment and perhaps he should have taken a booth instead.

The man swivels and once again faces the old woman and the snake. The reptile glances over at him, its forked tongue darting out repeatedly. It's not happy about the audience. But it's unwilling to break with decorum and attempt to snack on the voyeur, for the snake also knows it's not yet prepared to deal with the repercussions of such an attack.

On the table between them, placed with the same precision, are two settings of coffee. Occasionally the old woman draws the cup up to her brightly painted lips but she never quite makes contact.

"Drink up, my dear. Your coffee isss getting cold." The constrictor gently chides her but its yellow eyes are on the man.

The old woman still hesitates, however, as her eyes are drawn into the cup's contents: swirling in its murky depths, tiny pink worms, like ancient sea dragons, leap and dive – splashing with great zeal. Reading their movements, the misfortune teller nods in grim understanding. Still, she doesn't drink.

The man watches this little ritual with some interest and amusement. Eyes locked on those of the snake, he raises his cup in salute, but he doesn't take a sip, either. The snake bows its head slightly in the man's direction. It hisses quietly at the old woman, but loud enough so the man can overhear it.

"Jussst becaussse that obessse tabby isss a mafia kingpin, it doesssn't mean it getsss to put itsss whisssskery nossse in everyone'sss busssinessssss."

"Hush my dear. I really wish you'd forget about that incident with the Don. You didn't lose that – "

"I lossst *enough*. It'sss alwaysss – "

"Hush. All is not as it seems. I have seen – The Wyrms, they – perhaps it's best if we go right now."

The constrictor trusts her judgement and, gathering up their things, they do so without leaving a tip.

The man shrugs and turns back to face the counter.

"That's some coffee."

The waitress doesn't acknowledge the comment. She's busy setting up a small appliance, similar to a microwave. It's covered with bits of wire in a multitude of colors, and it has a glass door with a brass handle on the front. The waitress takes out a small silver fork attached to a fine chain around her neck and unlocks the door. She opens it, then places inside a cup which simply isn't shining enough to her standards. After closing and re-locking the door, the waitress disappears again under the table.

Moments later, she reappears wearing a heavy leather smock, gauntlets and a welding helmet. As she inserts the plug into the wall socket, she calls over her shoulder:

"I'd cover my eyes if I were you."

Then she throws the switch.

All vision is reduced to white.

If he were a lesser man he'd have gone blind. He'd also be extremely angered and annoyed that she gave him so little warning. Fortunately for both, he is himself, and his vision is almost immediately restored, if not sharper than before.

The waitress turns off the switch. Then she tilts her helmet back to actually see what she is doing. She opens the door to the appliance and carefully raises the glowing cup in her palms.

Her sigh is rapturous. "Ahhhhhh! Now that's better. Much better, indeed."

The cup shines with its own light. The waitress turns it in her gloved hands, inspecting it from every angle. Finally satisfied, she returns it, as well as the other items, to their respective places under the counter. Afterwards, she quickly looks in a nearby mirror scrutinizing her appearance, smoothing out her dress, picking off bits of lint. Then she runs her fingers across her tightly pulled back hair – making sure each sandy strand is still in place.

The man toasts her performance. "This sure is some great coffee." But the cup never reaches his lips.

Uncomfortable with the compliment, the young woman is hesitant with her reply. Trembling.

"You must understand that I only operate the mechanisms here which provide the coffee. I have my responsibilities. I provide a service. No more. No less. I cannot allow qualitative judgements to hold sway over me. It's too much – "

She is almost in tears.

"Please." The man almost reaches out, but she keeps her distance. "You are . . . I am . . . No more. No less." He smiles and she is drawn inside. Balanced. Warmed. Understanding. She returns his smile with equal warmth.

"Would you like a refill?"

"Oh . . . no, thank you. I never have more than one cup a day, but thank you very much just the same."

Somewhat dubious, she glances down at his cup. It is indeed coffee-less. The Wyrms remain, beyond death, waiting to be read – to serve their purpose and be set free.

Again uneasy, she clears her throat and barely manages: "Uh, you haven't quite finished."

Beatific, the man gently passes his palm over the cup. It's now empty.

"I have seen enough. It's not my intention – "

She's almost in shock. "But how can you – "

"Patience. More will come to light. We haven't even met yet. I don't wish to color anything much more than it needs to be. I should be on my way."

The man stands and draws a small handful of freeze-dried fish scales out of his pocket. Without a second glance, he places them on the counter and turns to go.

He calls over his shoulder: "Keep the change." And he's out the door before she can even think of something else to say. She doesn't try to follow, accepting her lot.

Outside, the memory complete, his surroundings are as they exist when he meets the young woman for the first time. The shops are empty of people as well as properties. Everything is worn and dilapidated. Gray and brown pre-dominate where there was once nauseating Technicolor. Dark, heavy clouds filled with acid rain loom above. Shadows living, dead, and otherwise surround him. He's almost up to his knees in waste at times and beyond his nostrils in stench. But he has other concerns.

The man resists the powerful urge to look back at the coffee-shop, knowing it'll be no better than anything else around him. Deeply saddened, he returns the way he came and contemplates his next move. Shop windows pass by, still calling for his attention. Surrounded by a long-dead neon coat hangar, a sign proclaims:

HUBRIS' DRY-CLEANING
ABORTION CLINIC
And
TAXIDERMY

Another one nearby states:

MAMMOTH UNDERTAKING
ROOFING
FLOWER ARRANGING
And More

This one has an elaborate legend written across the top of the window pane:

"For the best preserves and pigs' feet
you've ever had."

The man won't be drawn into their emptiness, however, and simply passes by every shop without slowing his pace. Soon he's met by the obese tabby, which is languidly stretched out on the stone steps leading up to a brownstone apartment. Its tail dances with the grace of a charmed cobra, as it tilts its head back and exaggerates a yawn.

The man stops below it. He sweeps off the garbage on a lower step, then eases himself down.

"That's quite the memory you have."

"And it's in Technicolor, too. Not as elegant as black and white, mind you, but I consider myself to be quite privileged."

The man nods. "As well you should."

"Had some fun with it though, I imagine?"

"Certainly. It's rare indeed for me to indulge myself, so why not?"

"Most assuredly. I'm glad I could be of help, and that you enjoyed reliving my memory, but in your own way, of course . . . Would you care to share your experience back with me?"

"By all means."

And the man does so, replaying the experience directly into the feline's mind.

Moments later, the tabby is rolling on its back, laughing heartily.

"I almost forgot about the snake that day – its tongue has always been a little loose."

"It's still around?"

"Ah, but of course. Still carrying a grudge against me, but I'm not terribly concerned. And still has that terrible lisp, too. Often it's with the old woman, whom you've already met, but it has its own minor business to deal with. Don't concern yourself with them; unless you so choose . . . Ah, but the Mistress – "

"Yes."

"I told you, didn't I?"

"Yes."

The man picks at the bits caught in the obese tabby's fur while it stretches itself back along a step. Then he firmly rakes his fingers along the cat's soft, ample belly. Purring deeply, the obese tabby melts under the man's touch. It takes more than a minute before the feline can compose itself enough to continue. Of course, it makes sure that the man keeps scratching in all the right places before it does so.

Rumbling: "You could go farther back, but I believe, if I remember correctly, it'll be more of the same. However, I must admit I had very few dealings with the Mistress then, so I may not be the best one to – "

"No. I've seen enough." The man slowly stops scratching. Sits forward. Elbows on his knees. Thoughtful. Melancholy.

Somewhat reluctantly, the obese tabby sits up and leans towards him.

"So, you understand then why she is so special to me? Among other things, she *knows* her responsibilities, and –"

"She does at that. Definitely unique. No need for a further explanation . . . But I still have a great deal to consider before I claim The Prize."

"You know that's not really necessary, but as you wish . . . as you wish . . . Shall we return then?"

"Certainly."

They both stand, regarding each other for a moment, then casually brush themselves off. Eyes sharp in the darkness, they make their way down the cluttered sidewalk to the obese tabby's hotel.

Their silence is more than companionable.

THE SENTINEL OF MYTH

Forenoon. Brunch. Well, for a few, anyway, a very select few. For most, their lives are like the sky: dull gray and brown, with little hope of any heavenly body. Only varying shades of darkness allow people to distinguish between day and night. But those select few, like the obese tabby, still enjoy their tea and sugar cookies right about now. As always.

And again, for others, it's another story – a different kind of time, a different kind of snack. Goons, in scraps of denim and leather, lots of polyester, and a lucky few with 100% cotton, stand on opposite sides of an alleyway. Waiting. Hairless. Featureless. Faceless. Literally. Everything removed to preserve their anarchistic anonymity; including their eyes, their teeth, and the skin on their hands. Built-in radar/sonar – like bats, only better, much better – keep them on edge, keep them alive. Waiting. Pipes, boards, knives, or shards of steel or of glass in their gloved hands. Waiting. Scars, scorn envelops them. Hungry. Waiting.

Waiting.

Footsteps.

Distant.

Approaching.

Arrival.

Presence.

The Goons quickly, but cautiously, form a circle around their quarry. But only because this so-called "quarry" allows them to do so. In the center, the figure draws a smile across cracked and rotting lips exposing brown hourglass teeth. Also dressed in rough and worn gray leather, but bearing no resemblance to the Goons, the figure lightly taps his fingers across his wasted chest, from which hang a multitude of tools: pliers, screw drivers, saw blades, and more. Across his back: a massive antique oak wood lathe and a small leather pack filled with more hardware and other delights. On his narrow hips, well-oiled and ready to rock: a crowbar on one and his favorite pump-action nail puller on the other. Waiting.

The figure turns casually, his smile never wavering, watching for the initiator. The Goons are poised. Alert. Committed, but terrified.

Finally, one leaps forward, hockey stick held high and back, ready to fly. With practiced ease, the figure's right hand whips out from his chest – a jigsaw blade seeks home in the Goon's throat. The impact knocks him back and he dies before his head hits the garbage-strewn asphalt.

The others cry out inarticulately and rush the figure – any previous strategies immediately forgotten. Without any unnecessary motions, the figure dispatches all comers – even those that quickly choose to run away. Far less than a minute passes before the figure stands amongst a score of the dead.

Serene, the figure balances what appears to be a complex level on his right index finger. All is as it should be. He pockets his art, then moves to each corpse and retrieves his wares, carefully wiping off all blood, brain, and bone. All are accounted for; so he tips his battered Stetson and moves onward.

Leaving the alleyway behind, he makes his way down a sidewalk – although, there is little difference between the two. Everywhere there is refuse – almost up to his knees at times – and that's saying a lot, considering how tall the figure is. Despite his great height, the stench still reaches him, but he has smelt worse. Much worse. Eyes forward, he continues. No great architecture to admire, no open and stocked shops with anything to tempt him. All is wasted and abandoned.

Except for one. Sandwiched between two towers of aluminum and Plexiglas, a small single-story cottage stands. No stone. No steel. All wood: brightly painted, warm glow inside, somehow *alive*, calling to him like a neglected mistress. Flowerbeds flourish. Shrubs and grass trimmed with care. A white picket fence lines the perimeter, with a gate down the middle, and a cobblestone path leads up to the porch. Intrigued, but resolute – business first – he moves onward, but not before snapping off a bunch of lilacs from one of the small, groomed trees near the fence. Inhaling deeply, he is momentarily intoxicated, and gains an extra spring in his step as he makes his way along the sidewalk.

Eventually, the figure reaches his destination, a tall, old brownstone hotel, recently re-named THE SCRATCHING POST. At the top of the stairs, the burly but ragged doorman stands – dressed in faded blue today. He waits to toss the figure back down, or open and then close the door at just the right moment – to keep the hot side hot, the cool side cool, and the redolence always on the outside. *And the vermin?* Well, that's a matter of opinion. That's to be seen, perhaps.

Without pausing, the figure ascends. As soon as he reaches the top step, the burly, but ragged doorman smiles politely, bows slightly, and maintains eye contact throughout their exchange. Pulling the door open, he greets the figure:

"You're expected in the coffee-shop, sir."

The figure returns the smile, tips his hat, and then enters. The door is eased shut behind him and he is left in the soft, warm, lemony glow of the lobby. Here too, everything is worn and dilapidated – wood cracked and rotten, paint fading, more verdigris than brass – but at least it's considerably cleaner than outside. No one is at the front desk, or anywhere else to be seen; so the figure crosses the vast room and heads for the coffee-shop.

Inside, the room is thick with spice and little else. Tables and chairs remain – some still upright and functional – but here too there is no one; well, except for the obese tabby sitting at a corner table. Set before it is a heaping plate of sugar cookies, a bone china tea set, a bowl of herbs, and a couple of half-empty milk shakes.

"Greetings!" The cat begins. "Welcome! Have a seat. Join me. Please." And it gestures towards a chair on the opposite side of the table.

The figure remains at the entrance.

"Nice reception."

The obese tabby beams. "Thank you. Nothing too extravagant, of course. I know you don't like all that fanfare for yourself. Besides, it's tea time; although, I still can't resist a good milk shake, as you well – wait. You mean the Goons in the alleyway, don't you?"

The tabby is met only with a smile. Then: "It's a good thing I'm ambi-dextrous."

"Pshawh. What was that – a minute of your time? Less? Probably rather anti-climactic at that, I imagine. Besides, I was doing both of us a favor. I know quite well that you would've been insulted if there had been no one whatsoever to challenge you. And as for myself, they weren't my men any-way – my cells were becoming overcrowded, and I didn't feel like bargain-ing with the other Dons for them, so I gave these perfect disposable hench-men a choice: a swift execution, or you – "

"A swifter one."

"They had no real idea, of course, but no matter. In the end, it's good PR for everybody involved."

"True enough."

"So please . . . have a seat."

The figure crosses the room and holds out the bunch of lilacs. The tabby accepts them graciously.

"So you've been by The Garden of Earthly Delights?"

The tabby places them in a milk shake, and the flowers open even more. Their fragrance fills the air.

"I thought that was the place – from what I've heard anyway. I've never actually been there before myself."

"Well then, after we're done our tea and chit-chat, you really must return. It's truly the ultimate in perversity and self-gratification: the most expensive and the most exquisite brothel around. But please . . ." The tabby waves toward the chair.

The figure removes his lathe and pack from his back and places them on a nearby chair. As he sits he drops his battered Stetson on a clear spot on the table. Then, he pours himself some steaming tea.

"Did the man go there?"

The cat pauses, swallowing uncomfortably.

"But of course – it was one the things that kept him here, I believe. He ran up quite a tab for me."

"Then we shall see. I'm not certain if I'll have the time, but – "

"Pshawh. Even if you can't stay long enough to indulge yourself, at the very least, you should take a quick tour. And whatever you decide, consider it my treat."

"That's extremely generous of you. Thank you."

"It's truly my pleasure . . . Catnip?"

"No. Thank you."

The obese tabby nibbles a little, then slurps on one of the milk shakes.

"Ahhhh! Black licorice. *The best*. You should try some. All natural ingredients. No preservatives. I could have one whipped – "

"How long was the man here?"

"He arrived a short time ago, perhaps a fortnight. Less . . . yes, less."

"And his works have been victorious in The Fray?"

"Yes. I'm sure you have heard – it defeated my Gronk." The tabby shakes its head sadly.

"My sympathies." The figure toasts the tabby.

" . . . Thank you . . ."

"Where is he now?"

"The man? Well, he was staying right here, in The Presidential Suite in fact, but he left just yesterday."

"Indeed?"

"Yes. His works have mostly healed and he finally claimed The Prize. And now he has moved onward."

"You didn't try to keep him here longer?"

"He is my Nemesis – so what can I say? I extended every hospitality, and we sometimes spoke at great length, learning about each other and our respective realms. To a certain degree, anyway. Well, actually I did most of the talking. In any case, I did what I could, and he seemed to be in no hurry. He didn't even claim The Prize until just before he left. There again, we missed out on some lovely promotion – there was no time for fanfare either, or even simply to gather the media."

"*Really?* That quickly?"

"Yes. That quickly."

"He didn't go back to his own realm though, did he?"

"He certainly didn't go that way, and in fact no one else has come from there since he first arrived. He may have even sealed off that entrance, but I haven't bothered to have it investigated yet. To be honest, I haven't been too concerned. All has gone well so far, so I thought it best not to tamper with anything."

"That's wise . . . Where was he last seen then?"

"Well, I understand he passed through *Ye Olde Wonkey Shoppe*, and into The Carnival. Then my people lost track of him in the masses."

The figure sips his tea. "Indeed?"

"Well, some say they saw him last enter The Funhouse, others, The House of Mirrors. Still others – but I'm sure you get the idea. The point is, no one saw him leave, but he *is* gone."

"Truly?"

"There has been no sign of him whatsoever. No clues. And he is not one to hide, or to go slinking about in the shadows, I'm sure . . . No, he's definitely gone. I must say, he's more formidable than I had ever imagined – a very worthy Nemesis, to say the least."

"But not without his weaknesses?"

"But of course. Who is not?" The tabby nods toward the lilacs.

"Truly, but tell me."

"He cares. He's curious. And he indulges occasionally in nostalgia."

"That much?"

"I have observed all of this, and more."

"Then I will find him."

"And then?"

"And then . . . we shall see."

The figure drains the cup, then gazes momentarily into the bottom and smiles.

The cat reaches for the teapot. "Another cup?"

"No. I should be on my way."

"So soon?"

"I would have another, but I'd like to take you up on your offer before I'm on my way."

"But of course. Shall I walk with you?"

"No, enjoy your brunch. Please."

"I'll inform the madam and let her know that you're to be expected."

"Thank you . . . for everything . . . I will not forget all that you've done for me."

"I'm sure you won't."

Hand in paw, they shake briefly, but warmly. Then the figure takes up his items and he is gone.

Soon afterward, he is once again before the cottage. Making his way along the cobblestones, he admires the freshly cut green grass, the variety of flowers, and the overall beauty of the setting, especially in regards to its surroundings. He steps onto the porch and over to the large door with a stained glass window set in the upper half. It is a seemingly abstract piece in a variety of colors, but the figure soon reads the underlying message.

Stepping back, he reaches over and pulls on the silken cord, which rings a bell inside and out. It's the first sound he hears from within the cottage. Almost immediately, the door is silently swung open, and the figure is met by a very short, very round, jovial, almost ancient woman, wearing pearls, a brightly patterned knee-length cotton dress, and knitted slippers. Antique pewter framed glasses hang around her neck, and her long white hair is pulled back into a tight bun and held in place with silver hairpins topped with tiny butterflies.

She beams. "Good day to you, sir. You've been expected. Please come in."

The figure removes his hat and bows slightly to the madam. Then he steps inside and the madam eases the door shut behind him. As with the exterior, the interior is very clean and well cared for. He takes a deep breath and, oak and lemon oil, rose and lilac, coffee and gingerbread, beeswax and peppermint welcome him. Around him is an assortment of furniture and art that in any other setting would never match. But here, they have been set with love and matronly charm; so it doesn't matter that priceless oil paintings hang beside velvet cats, or crystal vases with ceramic horses, or cherry wood chairs with bean bag ones.

All is aglow, but without electricity. Candelabra stand, chandeliers hang, sconces rest. All aflame, but it's never too warm.

"Can I take anything for you – to make your stay with us more comfortable?"

"I'm fine for the moment, but thank you."

" . . . I understand you're a carpenter?"

The figure grins. "Something like that."

"How nice . . . And this is certainly the place to be constructive." She gestures towards the bar. "Would you like something to drink? We have only the finest: freshly ground coffee, herbal tea, hot chocolate made from whole milk and melted white and milk chocolate, freshly squeezed orange juice, and the finest first choice of our patrons: ice cold spring water."

"The spring water, please."

"Certainly."

He accepts the topped off crystal goblet and holds it up to the chandelier, inspecting the water's clarity. Moments later, he swirls, sniffs, sips, slurps, but does not spit. Rather he swallows quite contentedly, then swallows another mouthful, but much more simply this time.

The figure sighs. "Like drinking it right from a mountain stream." He finishes the goblet and replaces it on the table.

"How right you are . . . We serve only the finest."

"To be sure. May I see more? I'm not certain what I would like yet, or if I'll actually take the time and – "

"Always a pleasure – which is also one of our mottoes . . . Please. This way."

She leads him from the front room down a long hall with doors spaced intermittently on either side: some opened, some closed. As well, there is a vast staircase leading both up and down several floors.

"We serve a rather elite, discriminating clientele, but you know how things go – with others reaching out, up and beyond their means. However, it's not for us to judge them, so rather than turn them away, we have expanded, as you can see for yourself. As well, as you've noticed you can either have complete privacy, or you can be part of any number. Take this room for example."

The madam gestures inside a vast sitting room where a number of finely dressed men sit on high back chairs watching one of the madam's finest. Attired in a full-length bathrobe and soft fuzzy slippers, with her long auburn hair in large curlers, she sits in a rocking chair knitting a sweater. Rocking slowly, evenly, her needles click lightly, and she stays focused on her work.

All of the patrons are transfixed, positively aglow. Some smile in glee, while the figure can hear at least one man muttering to himself.

"Oh yessss . . . twirl it, baby . . . around the needle and through and . . . yessss . . . yessss . . . do it again . . . slower this time . . . Slow-err . . ."

The figure raises an eyebrow and the two move on.

"Or perhaps this is more to your liking."

The madam crosses the hallway and points to a different room, where another hostess in a white blouse, cashmere sweater and a soft flowing skirt reads to a group of men sitting together on the floor before her.

"Or this."

Before an equally captive audience, a quartet of women in full-length, black silk gowns play: violin, viola, cello, piano.

"Or this."

Painting.

"Or this."

Writing.

"Or this."

Counting grains of sand.

"Or this: one of our games' rooms. More interactive with our hostesses: one on one or two on two or as the case may be." Checkers, chess, backgammon, billiards, foosball, darts, cards. "Perversions like these are rarely indulged in elsewhere. Especially with the skill level and imagination involved in some of these activities."

"Indeed."

"But for those who lack the skill but still have the funds, or for those who simply prefer to remain anonymous, we do provide many private rooms, and several carefully concealed entrances. And what goes on behind those closed doors . . . well, I'm sure you understand."

"Truly. Your reputation is very well-deserved."

"Thank you." They now stand in an archway leading into the dining room. "Would you care for anything?"

Spread across the massive table is a vast assortment of freshly baked cakes, cookies, dainties, pies, and pastries. Stacks of peanut butter and jelly sandwiches stand alongside bowls heaped with crab apples, wild blueberries, raspberries, and strawberries. Small cucumbers, young cobs of corn, carrots with their tops, and peas still in the shell wait to be cracked open. All this and more wait to be consumed.

The figure's eyes widen, taking in everything, momentarily wanting it all, but then feeling the absolute need to share. There is plenty for everyone.

"It's all so tempting."

In the end, however, he decides to hold himself back. He doesn't wish to indulge himself too much too soon. Must maintain focus. Then later, perhaps . . .

"That's our business, and your pleasure."

"Truly. I understand why the man was so fond of your establishment."

The figure notices the madam's hesitation. He continues, rather than waiting for her reply.

"Is there more?"

Somewhat relieved, the madam beams.

"Certainly. Through here and past the kitchen."

They weave their way through the enormous room, keeping out of the way of all the cooks and servers, who are happily scurrying back and forth. Prepping and cleaning. Cooking and baking. Filling orders. Having tiny samples. Making sure everything is just right. The figure breathes deeply the whole time, savoring every delicious scent and spice.

On the steps leading down, the figure pauses in amazement as he takes in the overwhelming beauty brightly lit before him. To his left, there is a vast vegetable garden, and to his right, an equally large and impressive flower and herb garden. All is abloom, rich and vibrant with life. Everything is lovingly tended by the brothel's patrons while several hostesses oversee their work. A variety of fruit trees line the perimeter and stretch off beyond his sight, which is saying a lot. The two follow the path, past the gardens and into a more secluded sylvan area. Here, men and woman play badminton, croquet, lawn darts, hide and seek, and some simply sit in the shade or swim in the spring-fed pool.

The figure's eyes follow the spring winding up into the distance and eventually up along a tree-covered mountain. The peak is hidden behind clouds of eider down and the figure attempts to see through them, but cannot.

"When was the man here last?"

Again, the madam hesitates. "Two days ago."

The figure turns to her, raising an eyebrow. "Not yesterday – before he left?"

"No. Not to my knowledge."

He considers her reply for a moment, then: "I understand he was last seen at The Carnival."

"That's what I've heard."

"But he didn't come back here? Perhaps through one of your secret passages?"

The figure glances at the cottage, which from this side looks more like a massive colonial mansion. Not surprised, he sharply surveys the area, but finds no clues.

"It's possible, but like I've said, not to my knowledge."

"Well, he *could have* disappeared into The Funhouse, or into The House of Mirrors, or into a score of other amusements, but this seems to be much more to his liking – his style."

"Perhaps. But I wouldn't be too quick in judging him."

"Indeed . . . Nonetheless, I believe he is here, somewhere . . ."

The figure turns about slowly, searching, but knowing he will see no indication of the man's passage.

"You're not – "

"I make no accusations. I simply believe that he has come this way, and he will return . . . I understand only too well his attraction for your establishment. Besides, he still has unfinished business with the obese tabby, I'm sure."

He crosses over to an ancient oak, pulls off his wood lathe and his pack, and sits back against the trunk. The madam follows at a short distance, feeling uncertain, but only somewhat afraid. She doesn't sit with him.

Aware of her unease, the figure smiles, but to little effect.

"So here I will remain."

"And then?"

"And then – " The figure puts on his battered Stetson, and eases the brim over his eyes. "– we shall see."

MIRROR LICKERS ANONYMOUS

Midnight. Heavy hand swinging down to start a new day. How delightful. As always.

The people gather, carrying their misfortune close to their hearts in sacks of paper, plastic, canvas, and burlap. Glass, steel, and wire poking through – searching, expanding. Almost alive for some, transcendental for others. Waiting.

The throng mills about the alleyway, near a loading dock. Waiting. Clicking, cackling, humming, hissing, spinning, spitting, ticking, talking, whirring, whirling. Waiting. For someone else to make a move. Waiting. To be taken care of. Waiting. Complacent but still complaining. Waiting. As always. Waiting.

Waiting. Speaker yet unseen. Unknown. Last week's is already here, but he's not about to step forward again. No way. No how. Not after their last gathering.

What's the point?

There should be one, or two, at least, since so many come around each time. But to make that leap from thought to expression; from rhetoric to revolution; that remains to be seen. No one has been able to accomplish these tasks yet, but again, no one has really tried. Everyone's self-absorbed, revolving in their individual microcosms, gravitating towards their own misfortune. Worshipping it. Existing for it. But still, there is a cultish sense of community – well, to a degree.

So, perhaps tonight will be different. Perhaps. But don't bank any big bone on it, just in case.

Eventually an entourage approaches. At its epicenter the speaker strolls, head held high above the others. But not for too long. He can't forget himself entirely, and he too is drawn inward – towards the canvas satchel resting on his hip. Hand caressing. Drawing comfort, confidence, conviction. A voice.

Hesitatingly, almost grudgingly, the mass parts for the entourage – still whining and bleeping, grimy and sleepy, diseased and delirious. Stepping ahead, the speaker takes the stairs and stands on the edge of the loading dock. Leaning. Peering into the shadows. Searching. Finally, finding eye contact in the shadows. A beginning, then another: first an old woman then a young one. He decides to go with youth, energy, naiveté, and he speaks to the young woman directly, quickly attempting to draw the others in – expanding, and encompassing everyone. But who knows for how long?

"Welcome! My friend . . . my friends . . . my brothers and sisters! Welcome! Your presence is much appreciated, and very understandable, given our circumstances. Yes! That's a good place to begin. *Our circumstances!* Yes! I have a question, which I'm sure you all know the answer to, but perhaps one of you would care to answer it aloud. And that is: whom do we have to blame for *our circumstances*? Who is responsible for *our circumstances*?"

The mob shuffles, scuffles somewhat. Murmurs. Finally, the young woman with whom the speaker first addressed, says in a shaky voice:

"Ourselves?"

Silence. Unease. Brief self-examination here and there. Then anger and righteousness. Fortunately for the young woman, it's too dark, and most of the people haven't been paying enough attention to know who spoke exactly; otherwise, she'd likely be pulled apart by now. Well, perhaps. They're as bloodthirsty as anyone and about as brave, so it's really hard to say. In any case, the speaker publicly ignores her response, but privately makes a note of her. He quickly moves onward.

"You know who I am talking about . . ."

"The obese tabby." A member of his entourage offers.

"Yes! The obese tabby! And even now it has – "

"Hey!" A voice calls. "I'd heard there was going to be free tea and sugar cookies that were left over from today's brunch. And I don't know about anyone else, but I don't see any tea and sugar cookies anywhere."

The speaker nods, and two of his flunkies head towards the teatime man. He escapes, however, as others awaken somewhat, and they make the henchmen's way difficult. Not that his flunkies are all that committed to begin with, but they have nothing else to do. The teatime man gone, his pursuers blend in with the crowd. Bored.

Many others cry out:

"Yeah! Where's the tea?!"

"Did you receive a pamphlet? I didn't."

"Get your hand out of my pockets!"

"Oh no! I think I lost my remote! Help me find it! Please! Please, help me!"

The speaker attempts to calm them, to retake control, but to no avail. Rather, the people become more frenzied. Most are babbling incoherently. Some strike out at anyone nearby. Others try to get on their own personal pedestal or soapbox, as the case may be.

"Who mourns for the dinosaur?!"

"Look at *meeee*! Look at *meeee*! See *myyyy* pain?!"

"You call *this* entertainment?!"

"This sucks! I'm going back to The Carnival."

Among them, bouncing person to person, the young woman shrieks:

"What of our responsibility?! I know mine! Do you know yours?! Oh, nobody takes the time any more. It's not for me to tell you, either, but do you know what it is? Do you?! I'm just asking . . . Disaster to those who take their possessions for granted!"

Inspired, the gaudily clad, haggard misfortune teller joins in:

"All is not as it seems! All is not as it seems! Let me show you your – "

But before she can say any more, the throng dissolves and she is swept away; eventually abandoned. Even the speaker's entourage has left him standing alone on the loading dock. Only the young woman remains before him, but her attention is elsewhere. She sits cross-legged among the refuse, her large canvas bag open in her lap. Humming.

The speaker is exasperated. "What's the point of a revolution – "

The young woman sings to herself, badly off-key, and the speaker looks down at her, but can't decipher the words, except for "general copulation." She suddenly stops singing. Smiles. Laughs maniacally. "Yes. I remember hearing that sung many times when I was a child . . . More born so that more can die. *And for what?* What is our responsibility? Hmmm?"

Head down, the young woman clears a space in front of herself. She draws out several pieces of glass and metal and begins to reverently assemble them on the asphalt.

Inspired, the speaker leaps down and stands before her, his military surplus shoulder bag in his hands. Ignored, he sits facing her and clears his own space, hissing and crackling throughout. Equally reverent, he opens his satchel and places its content piece by broken piece on the asphalt. Eventually both of their bags are empty and a mosaic composed of bits of glass, metal, plastic, wires, and circuits surrounds them.

Gazing into each other's eyes, they find a brief moment of tranquillity. Tentatively, they reach for each other but never make contact. They can't. It's not allowed. Instead, their arms drop and their gaze lowers to the mosaic around themselves.

Finding her voice again, the woman softly sings in a dry, deadpan manner. But again, badly off-key.

"Somebody made a mistake down at the factory.
This piece – it doesn't fit right

and that is not right.

It's too big on one end; too small on the other.
It doesn't fit no matter how we try.
Even its color is a little bit off.
It wasn't made for this puzzle at all."

The speaker joins in with her on the chorus; equally deadpan, but more on key.

"Somebody made a mistake down at the factory.
This piece – it doesn't fit right
and that is not right.

If it could be changed, then maybe it would work.
Who knows how to do it the way it should be done?
Jam the piece in there. We'll have to make due.
It won't be perfect, but it won't be wrong.
So we'd like to think.

Somebody made a mistake down at the factory.
This piece – it doesn't fit right
and that is not right."

The two stays seated, both staring at the street and at the remains of their misfortunes.

The speaker sighs. Glances up at her. "I haven't heard that song since I was a kid."

"Me neither. I don't even like it all that much, but it's the only song I remember all of the words for. I don't know when I first heard it, but I do remember when I was just starting as a waitress at Ego Sideroad's, and the song was banned . . . and how *they* came around and confiscated all of the recordings we had, including this one. I think that's what made me remember the words; although, I don't even know what they really mean."

"You're very special. Do you know that?"

"That's what I keep hearing, but I don't know if I'm being insulted or not."

"Well, not by me."

"Good." She hesitates, scanning his bearded face, his hard, sharp gray eyes. Then: "Have we met before?"

He considers her question, her presence.

"No . . . not like this."

"Like how then?"

"Like . . . not face to face . . . like . . . in my head . . . in dreams . . . or well, maybe nothing, I guess."

"Really? Well, you sure remind me of someone."

"Who?"

"Just a man passing through, looking for somewhere to stay. But he was older and a bit taller and didn't have a beard."

"I'm just passing through, too . . . Well, actually, I *was* passing through here a couple of weeks ago, but I've kind of got sidetracked."

"And where were you supposed to be going?"

"The desert."

"There's no desert around here."

"I know, I know. I zigged when I should have zagged, and I've been here for awhile, taking everything in, and trying to find my way; although, I must say I'm not in that much of a hurry to get to the desert anyway."

"I can understand that. Why go in the first place? Is that a part of your responsibility? Because you know, nobody seems to – "

"I'm a prophet."

"Really? Well, I suppose you kind of look like one, even though you really don't sound like one – "

"Yeah yeah yeah – I know, I know, that's the whole problem. I'm no good at this, but I'm pretty much stuck with the gig. So I figured I'd go and put in forty days and forty nights – sweating it out, having some visions, fighting some demons, resisting a few temptations, and in the end just hope for the best."

"I see."

"You probably don't, but that's OK."

"Are you *sure* that we haven't met before?"

"Yeah."

The woman pauses, glancing down and taking in the pieces between them. Her eyes widen, and a slow, sly smile spreads across her face.

"What is your misfortune, prophet?"

"That's a rather loaded question, isn't it?"

"What's between us then?"

"Ditto."

"Ditto?"

"Yeah. Same answer to your question, or rather, same question to your question."

The woman laughs hysterically, shrugging off his explanation.

"Well, let me tell you that this – " She gestures grandly with both arms, palms upward, her fingers splayed; her lucidity lost. "– is what remains of my microwave, which once possessed some rather convenient, but also startling properties . . . Top of the line! Oh yes! Top of the line!"

The speaker captures her fever, her rapture. He extends his arms and cracks his knuckles, then displays his own misfortune just as impressively.

"Well, this – my dear, young woman – is what remains of my portable stereo, which also once possessed some rather innovative, but also frightening qualities . . . Buy now, pay later!"

Eyes wildly insane, she challenges: "Well then, shall we see what we can whip up together then?"

"A singing microwave?"

"Oh, perhaps. And more. Much more I'm sure."

"Another song then as we work?"

She considers this, then: "You'll have to teach me."

The prophet sighs, delighted. "You don't know how long I've been waiting for someone to say that to me."

"Hmph?"

"For me to teach someone something, *anything*!"

The young woman cackles, spittle flying.

"Well, poets and prophets ain't what they used to be. No sir, let me tell you . . . but at least you know your responsibility . . . and I know mine. Oh yes!"

"Shall we begin then?"

The young woman starts drawing pieces together, humming in a whole new way, and the prophet quickly joins her, picking out a song:

"Nothing changes . . . Nothing changes . . ."

THE STONE REMAINS THE SAME

Gloaming. Once again. Diffused violet light slowly fading into black. The air is crisp on the mountainside where the man stands, peering into an even deeper darkness of a mineshaft.

He has climbed this far and he could go higher, but for how long? Physically he is prepared, but his suit and leather soled shoes are not exactly made for mountaineering. The man also has his small suitcase and umbrella to contend with, which do not make for two-handed climbing. Besides, he would much rather go through than over to reach the other side.

He steps inside, using his umbrella to help feel his way along. Soon light has no meaning, *and time?* Well, that's a different story altogether. But still, the man continues cautiously into the tunnel, his superior senses peaked.

Hours pass as he quietly winds his way through different tunnels, avoiding cave-ins, trip wires, and vertical shafts that are not quite bottomless. Inside, it's no less cool and the air is heavy with moisture. Occasionally it's also redolent with decay. He doesn't altogether avoid the sources of the varying degrees of odor. Rather, desiring some answers, he seeks out those that are along his way.

So feeling clammy and following his nose, the man finds the first body which is mostly buried under a cave-in. Carefully feeling his way around, he discovers that it's the body of an adult male, clean-cut, wearing a suit and tie. From the degree of decomposition, he roughly determines the body hasn't been there for more than a couple of weeks. The man searches the body for any identification then digs through the rubble, checking for personal effects, but finds nothing. Taking up his own items, he leaves the body and climbs over the mound.

A short while later, the man finds two more bodies – young men – and they too are dressed in expensive suits. Once again, however, they have no identification or personal effects. What they do have is a knife in each of their backs, which haven't been there for very long – for perhaps only a day or two. More cautious, but resolute to reach the other side, the man moves onward.

As time passes, the man finds more bodies. Some have been recently murdered, while others appear to be victims of misadventure and misfortune. As well, a great number are little more than skeletons. Most of the recent corpses are missing limbs and internal organs; including their brains, but never their hearts. All of the bodies are similarly attired, and almost all of them are men. No miners. No minors.

Occasionally, the man hears voices in the distance, sometimes crying out, but he doesn't investigate these sounds. He knows well enough that danger will find him if it wants to, as it has often enough in his past. The man is as prepared as he can be for any confrontation, but he prefers to go quietly through.

Eventually he sees a spot of light, which grows with each step he takes. As he draws nearer, he also hears what sounds like the braying and bleating of nervous or frightened sheep. In this final shaft, the rotting stench grows even though there are no more corpses to be seen. So the man steps carefully, his senses still alert for any more traps.

Soon he is at the end facing a revolving door, which is rotating smoothly. The thick glass distorts everything on the other side, which is gleaming in golden light. There is a great deal of movement and the cacophony of voices is barely tolerable, but the man distinguishes little. He waits for a few moments, allowing his eyes and ears to adjust. Then the man steps forward and he passes through.

His eyes become narrow slits as he crosses over, still adjusting to the overwhelming brightness. Even though there are no obvious sources of light, all is shining brilliantly. All of the walls, the floor, and the fixtures are made of polished precious metals – gold, silver, and platinum – and they appear to be radiating with a light of their own. Many of the features are also high-lighted with gemstones, such as diamonds, emeralds, rubies, and sapphires.

The man surveys everything around him, although it gives him a small headache to do so. Standing in this massive lobby, he takes in the portraits etched in silver lining the walls from floor to ceiling, several stories high. As well, there are life-size golden statues of other immaculately dressed businessmen spaced at wide intervals along the perimeter. All of the renditions are extremely serious but sinister. Sharp eyes. Sharper teeth. Grim, but greasy smiles. Greasier palms. Young and slick. Old and wily. Always hungry and never satisfied.

In between each of the portraits are engraved lists of names: employees of the month, those killed in the line of duty, and other honorees and retired individuals. In the center of the lobby is an ornately carved pewter fountain, lined with crystal and topped with the platinum CEO. He is holding a vice in one hand and a champagne bottle in the other, from which refined oil is flowing. Behind the fountain a short distance away is a raised reception desk area, where several men and women are keeping nervously busy, just like everyone else around the man. All are attempting to rush across the packed lobby, to and from elevators and side doors, holding quick conferences before they disappear.

Despite the arena-like size of the lobby and the movement of the suits, there is little airflow as there is no air conditioning of any kind. All of the colognes, aftershaves, and perfumes hide nothing – sweat and blood, halitosis and flatulence, excrement and gangrene. The lobby is a corral. Period. *And the abattoir?* Pick a door on any floor . . . any door at all.

Moving casually along, the man focuses on specific individuals, and he's able to capture some of the suits' conversations.

From one:

"That's exactly why we're closing the factory down. We didn't expect to make our money back so quickly. If it had made it more slowly, even taking ten years, we'd keep it open. But we have our investment back, so we don't need it any more. And what's ten thousand people out of work . . . really?"

To another:

"I don't care that you made five million gross in the last quarter. What concerns me is that you only sold twelve items at $417,000 to make that amount. *Think of your Items Per Man Hour!* You should have sold 1.2 million at $4.17. Or twelve million at forty-two cents each. Now *that* would impress me."

And another:

"Don't you even *think* of trying to fix it yourself. Do you have any idea how well gold conducts electricity? Well, I don't exactly, but remember the last exec that tried to repair his terminal? He got a couple of wires crossed and when he plugged the terminal back in, he fried himself and half the people here. Now *that* was a barbecue and a half."

And so on.

The man has heard enough and, from what he sees as well, he realizes that in some ways he has made a mistake in coming here. Nonetheless, he doesn't turn back to the revolving door, as there is still more he can learn. As he approaches the reception desk, he continues to observe those around him.

Most of the people are unshaven and unwashed, with their suits rumpled and torn, and some are burned. Almost all of them are starving and many even appear to be beyond death. Initially the man believes it's a trick of the lighting, but he quickly realizes that he can actually see through many of the people. However, these ghostly figures are treated no differently than anyone else – including the zombies and ghouls rotting away – so the man pays them no more attention than the others do.

Many of the suits are also missing limbs: hands, arms, feet, legs. The handicapped use crude canes and crutches – such as golf clubs, *lots* of golf clubs – and makeshift prosthetics. Broken skis, blocks of wood and foam padding from chairs, and duct tape are used for feet and legs; tennis racket handles for forearms, with home-made hooks, rubber stamps, and pens for fingers.

Finally through the great mass, he reaches the reception desk. The man waits for quite some time while those on the receiving side hold a conference, draft up various proposals, and then hold a secret ballot to decide who will help him. As the hour ticks by, the man decides to strike up a conversation with the young suit waiting in line behind him.

"What brings you here?"

Startled at being acknowledged so quickly the young suit stammers:
" . . . uh . . . job interview." He holds out his hand, suddenly uncertain if this is someone who is to pre-question him and to possibly catch him off guard.

The man shakes the slick, sweating palm firmly, not allowing it to slip through his fingers. Locking his eyes on the young suit, he nods once, and then lets go. He doesn't introduce himself, which causes greater fear and suspicion within the young suit. Then the man discreetly wipes his palm on his long coat, knowing it needs a good cleaning anyway. The young suit is too nervous to notice the gesture; not that it would matter too much to the man if he did.

"So you're new here as well?"

The young suit doesn't buy the man's honesty, being largely unfamiliar with the concept. He can't believe the man could possibly be *new* anywhere, especially *here*. Still, he answers, hoping to score well.

" . . . Just graduated . . . third of twelve . . . Uh, by the way, sorry to be late, but I got lost in the tunnels for awhile. Ha."

"Understandable." The man pauses briefly, then: "Of twelve? Really?"

"Yes. Extremely exclusive . . . solely established with the intention of moving on to here . . . if one meets the requirements, of course. Only the absolute best, as I'm sure you know only too well."

"So Number One and Number Two are already here then?"

The young suit darts his eyes around. Apprehensive. Barely shrugs.

"I, uh . . . wouldn't know."

The man makes a point of catching the young suit's eyes again and he holds him in his place. Keeps him sweating. Trembling. Profusely.

"Of twelve and you don't know where your friends have moved on to-wards?"

The young suit continues to shake, trying to unlock the man's fierce gaze. He's on the verge of a seizure, but he finally explodes.

"I killed them alright! In the tunnels on the way here! Friends?! Ha!"

Breaking contact for a moment, the man searches around quickly. Many others heard the young suit, but no one stops. They've heard it all before. Par for the course. Plenty more where they came from. One is much like another. Cliche after cliche. The man, however, is not quite so uncaring. He looks back at the babbling young suit.

"I did what I had to – we were all up for the same position. You would've done the same. You probably have many times, so don't judge me. I may've been third of twelve once, but look at me now. You don't see the other two, now do you? So much for the competition. Ha!"

The man regards him relentlessly. "Look around you, *boy*. What do you see?"

Shifting his eyes around the lobby, the young suit is almost rapturous.

"Expeditious, industrious people who've made it! Wealth! Power! All theirs, and soon to be all mine!"

"Really? Nothing more?"

The young suit pauses, confused. Then he searches for a different angle, hoping to give the correct response.

" . . . Well, uh . . . Everyone makes sacrifices, and not everyone can be on top."

"True enough. How many managers can dance on the head of a pin?"

"I don't . . . I . . ."

"Who do you serve?"

"That's easy: myself."

"Who do you love?"

"Well that one, I never . . ."

The man continues to fire questions at the young suit, well aware he's not really getting through to him, but still he has some hope. Some time later he feels a tap on his shoulder, and turns to find one of the people behind the reception desk has come forward. Before he can talk with her, however, the young suit draws him back with a question of his own.

"So did I get the job? Ha?"

The man sighs. "I wouldn't hire you, but it's not for me to decide."

Feeling dubious, but glad he hasn't been sent away, the young suit remains standing behind the man, hoping he has passed the first test; not counting killing Number One and Number Two. He waits for his turn at the reception desk, trying to listen in on the man's conversation, expecting to hear something about his "Pre-interview."

"How can I help you, sir?"

Surrounded by mostly dead computer screens, a sallow-skinned, middle-aged woman leans across the high counter, her face creased with a scurvy smile. She reaches out with her dirty right hand to the man and holds a scanning baton in her left. As the man extends his own right hand he notices a bar code tattooed across the top of hers. Immediately he drops it, and hurriedly surveys those around him. Every right hand he sees has a similar tattoo, including the young suit's behind him. With all of the blood and grime, it never registered earlier. The man, of course, doesn't have this bar code; although, with all of his scars, the woman is not sure if she saw a tattoo or not, having only caught a glimpse of his hand.

Still holding out her hands to him, she no longer smiles. Petulant. Licking her bleeding gums in agitation, wanting to pick at the scurvy-blossoms on her face, she waits for his hand. The others behind her hold back expectantly, fastidiously doing a whole lot of nothing, while a line builds behind the young suit.

"Your hand please, sir. Then you can tell me your business with us. Others are waiting to be served."

The man doesn't move, but neither does he attempt to deceive her. Not exactly.

"I'm new around here."

"I see."

The woman drops her hands to the counter, with one lingering closely to the panic button. If there is any security left, she is uncertain, but the button gives her some comfort nonetheless. She pauses, throwing him a line.

"If you don't have a number on file with us, we can assign you one; otherwise we can't conduct any further business. So, just tell me your name, number, or designation, please, and we can begin with that."

"Whether or not you have a file on me, I don't know, but I don't wish to be assigned a number. Nor do I wish to reveal my name at this time. It wouldn't be prudent."

Hearing all this, the young suit steps back from the man, disassociating himself. He realizes that he's mistaken in the man's identity, but he can possibly earn some extra brownie points if he acts at just the right moment.

Meanwhile, the receptionist presses the panic button. There is no audible alarm, of course, so she only hopes there is still a connection and someone is on the way. Then, with professional dedication, she proceeds to question the man, intent on stalling him.

"Why are you trying to be difficult, sir?"

"I apologize. It's not my intention. I'm here on a simple errand, to do some business perhaps, largely involving The Prize, and for that – "

For a nanosecond the lobby is still and silent, then everyone carries on with their business.

"– I don't wish to involve myself in any unnecessary and possibly dangerous – "

The woman snaps up her hand, wishing she hadn't hit the button, stopping the man in the process.

She leans in, stage whispering: "You mentioned The Prize."

The young suit eagerly steps forward again, almost bumping into the man, who ignores him.

"Yes. My works recently defeated the obese tabby's Prime Enforcer in The Fray. I have The Prize with me now. I realize that I didn't make an appointment, but all things considered, I was hoping whoever was in charge would have a moment or two to meet with me."

The young suit draws closer, but is stopped by the man who turns on him. His eyes say everything, and the young suit flees in a terror of understanding out the revolving door. The man didn't wish to take matters so far with him, not believing it was his place to do so, but he has no regrets. Perhaps the young suit will take the time to change his life or, perhaps, in his flight, he will hit a trip wire or fall down a mineshaft. Whatever the case, the man is simply relieved that the young suit is gone from this place.

The man faces the receptionist again. She is typing rapidly on one of the keyboards while those behind her are rushing around trying to do the same. Only one other computer is working, however, although no one seems to notice this except the man. He refrains from making any comment.

The woman glances up at him, running her tongue across her gums.

"My apologies to you, sir. Had I known . . ."

She pauses, remembering the panic button. Fortunately, no one has arrived yet, nor does she believe anyone will at this point. She looks back at her monitor, chagrined.

"I'll just be a moment. I only have to . . . oh this . . . this . . . I'm sorry, sir. This new system was just recently installed. We had just worked out the bugs in the previous system and then it became obsolete almost immediately. They installed this one, but once again, we're not quite up to speed yet. And they're almost finished working on another new one in Research and Development to replace this one, since it's practically obsolete itself. Just can't keep up with technology these days. Although, truth be told, there was nothing much wrong with the first system they installed here long before I was ever around . . . Just another moment or two, sir."

The man shrugs. " . . . I've waited this long . . . but what exactly are you doing, anyway?"

"Oh, uh, trying to find someone who can guide you to the appropriate person, and I'm also trying to find out who the appropriate person is."

"Who's in charge?"

"Everyone is . . . well, in one way or another. There are so many departments, categories, sub-categories, districts, sub-districts, divisions, sub-divisions – "

"I understand."

"Well, I really don't, but it's not my job to understand, only to *receive*. . . uh, here we go."

"Now do I have to wait for someone? Can't you give me a floor and a room number?"

"Oh no. That's not permitted. Do you have any idea how many toes I'd be stepping on if I simply allowed you to go on your way?"

"Well then, can't *you* take me there?"

"The same rules apply, and I can't leave my post."

Just as the man is about to insist on her accompanying him, a spectral voice breaks over the intercom beside her monitor.

"It's alright. Please bring him to me."

All the receptionists freeze for a minute, then slowly thaw and return to life. The woman looks at her monitor one last time, memorizing what she needs to know, then clears it and steps away. Eyes wide. Haunted.

"Follow me, sir."

The receptionist crosses to the back gate where the man meets her. Together they move with many others to the elevators. Crammed inside of one, they go up to the top. Along the way, the man questions the receptionist, very aware of those around them, and that they are likely still being observed.

"I noticed that no one arrived after you hit the panic button. Was that *his* doing?"

Staring at the numbers flashing higher, the receptionist quivers. Despite other floor numbers being pressed, the elevator keeps passing them.

" . . . uh, possibly, sir . . . I don't really know much about such things."

"Really? Hmmm . . . Well, I must admit I haven't seen anyone that hasn't been wearing a suit here."

She remains silent, but still quivering. The suits around them grumble a little but stay out of their conversation.

"Is your security disguised?"

Nothing.

"Do your cleaners and maintenance crews only work after hours?"

Nothing.

"Do *after hours* even exist here?"

Nothing.

The man surveys those around him, checking if someone will answer him. Most are turned away: two are sniffing diamond dust, another is smoking a thousand dollar bill that has been soaked in petroleum, while several others are chewing on small bits of rotting meat – some from their own stumps.

"Do any of you possess any real skills, or are you all just a bunch of soulless managers endlessly crunching numbers?"

The elevator stops.

The receptionist manages to mutter: " . . . uh, here we are . . . sir."

The doors slide open on a dim corridor, the walls illusory. The two get off the elevator and the receptionist starts to lead the man through a smoky, shadowy, multilevel maze. They walk silently, any sounds dying immediately after their birth. Eventually they reach their destination, but the receptionist will go no further. Terrified, but determined to make it back to the reception desk, she scurries away without any parting words to the man.

The man knocks firmly on the nameless ebony door. Although the rapping is almost inaudible, a hollow voice calls from the other side.

"Please come in."

The man does so. Inside, he casts a curious eye around the spacious room. Here, it's no less shadowy or smoky. Along a wide perimeter, hundreds of small projections are cast against the smoke. Scenes from throughout the building, and elsewhere – offices, shops, bedrooms, the tunnels, and more – are plainly visible. The man glances briefly from screen to screen, then quickly loses interest.

Across from the man is an elaborately carved desk constructed of ivory and a captain's chair covered in several extinct animal skins. With the exception of a silver platter covered with thin strips of raw meat, and a tall golden goblet, the desktop is empty. The man steps up to the desk. Sniffs over the goblet. He doesn't even try to hide his disgust.

"Blood . . . Typical."

The man doesn't bother touching either offering. Steps back. Waits.

"Greetings." The spectral voice calls – not from the chair, but from all around the man. But the voice is subtle. Silvery. Slippery. Almost silent.

"Hello." The man pauses, looking around the room. "Is this the way we are going to do business? *If* we are going to do business?"

"But I am here."

Suddenly the man catches a glimpse across the room, barely a shadow and then nothing at all. Moments pass. Then he catches another glimpse of the spectral figure and feels a sharp chill emanating from him. Soon, the man is able to distinguish him from the surroundings most of the time, although it's actually easier for him to see the spectral figure when he's not directly attempting to do so.

The spectral figure takes his seat, then gestures for the man to have one himself. The man turns his head to see a similar chair appear. Setting his small suitcase beside the chair, he sits – not happy about the sources, but relieved to finally be off of his feet – his first time since he initially climbed the mountain.

The spectral figure begins: "So you have finally arrived. I am glad. And you have done very well for yourself. For that too, I am pleased."

"Thank you." The man gestures towards the screens. "You've followed me since the beginning?"

"Yes. Long before your arrival in the obese tabby's domain. So sorry to have kept you in the lobby for so long, but I rather enjoy watching you in action."

The man remains silent. The spectral figure pauses, then:

"Please have something. I know it does not seem like much, but I assure you that it is the best we have to offer. Those morsels taste just like pork. Honestly."

"That's not so surprising."

"No it is not actually . . . But please . . ."

"Thank you, but no, I'll get by."

"Alright. I will press the matter no further, but if you change your mind . . ."

"Certainly."

"Well then, I imagine you have many questions . . . and you have business to attend to . . . to deal with your Nemesis, the obese tabby . . . and then there is The Prize, of course."

The man nods. " . . . But from what I've seen recently, I'm uncertain – "

"Come now. Do not tell me you have come all this way, only to say that you are not interested in dealing with me."

"Perhaps I'm doing exactly that."

"And to make some observations and assessments of your own, I imagine? Feeling out the competition?"

"I imagine so."

"And so, what have you observed? What have you assessed?"

The man sighs. Stands, taking up his suitcase.

"I wish to go now."

"That says enough, I suppose. But if you will not deal with me, who then? The obese tabby may be very cordial, and it does like its catnip and licorice milk shakes a little too much, but do not underestimate it. It is not your Nemesis for nothing."

"I'll see what The Emperor has to say."

"The Emperor? Really? Will you be so audacious?"

"I do what I feel is necessary. Besides, everywhere I go people seem to be expecting me, so I imagine The Emperor is expecting me as well. . . So now I shall take my leave of you."

The man turns to go. The chair is gone, and the spectral figure is before him radiating absolutely arctic coldness. The man can't help but shiver a bit but, otherwise, he is calm, resolute. The spectral figure holds out his hands in supplication.

"Wait! Is it not possible for us to discuss these matters like gentlemen? Surely, you must be exhausted after such a long journey. I know you must be hungry . . . thirsty . . . I can have something else prepared . . . You will find it very empowering, very invigorating, I am sure . . . And besides, you need rest, like every man."

"Thank you for your courtesy, but I'm not exactly every man."

The spectral figure drops his hands, chagrined. He challenges: "Well, if you thought the journey here was treacherous, wait until you have to cross the desert."

"I've made it this far."

With that, the man walks around the spectral figure and out the door. The spectral figure does not follow him, except for on the screens, of course. Back in the maze, the man makes his way carefully along, well aware that he may not be intended to leave.

It takes him considerably longer to return to the elevator, but he does so, unscarred. As he arrives, the doors are already open, the elevator vacant. He steps inside and presses LOBBY. After a moment, the doors slide shut and he begins his descent. Once again, no stops are made along the way and, with only one passenger, the elevator accelerates rapidly, but nowhere near terminal velocity. Eventually it slows down as it reaches the lobby.

Stopped, the man waits for the doors to open, but nothing happens. Then, from behind himself, he hears doors unseal, and he turns to see a long, dark hallway. Walking casually down the hallway, the man passes several doors and side passages, but he doesn't deviate from his chosen path. As he goes by the gym, he slows to peer inside the large windows. Men and women, living and undead, work out their emaciated bodies, doing whatever exercises their limited limbs will allow. Mirrors line the other three walls floor to ceiling. Everyone is transfixed, only pausing to switch machines, or from barbells to dumb-bells, or to flirt as emptily as always. Almost immediately he has seen enough, so the man picks up his pace and makes his way for the exit. It's not clearly posted, but the man hopes it'll be at the end of this hallway.

Soon he's outside, under a cloudless azure sky, with no heavenly body to be seen, and with nothing but the desert before him. Feeling the heat on his back, he turns around to see that he is standing at the base of a pyramid constructed of bars of precious metals, which are shining brightly. Excruciatingly so.

The exit door has disappeared.

The man turns his back to the pyramid, glad to be finally free of it. He removes his tie, folds and pockets it, and unfastens the top two buttons of his shirt. Then reaching down, he draws up a handful of gold dust, and lets it fly into the wind. Following the trail in the air, the man chooses that to be the direction to find The Emperor. Hearing his stomach rumble, he opens his umbrella and takes his first steps.

JUST DESERT

Zenith. Yet, no sun, no clouds, no shadows cast. Only clear azure sky above, and seemingly endless golden sand stretching out in all directions. Dune after dune. And heat: perpetual, oppressive heat. So, zenith.

The man walks, just as he has walked for countless hours, the simoon at his back, hopefully directing him towards The Emperor's domain. But so far there are no signs of it.

. . . Nothing changes . . . Nothing changes . . .

Time continues to sift through, a grain at a time, but still it is no less bright, no less hot, and no more interesting than before.

Nothing changes.

Until, eventually, the man catches a glimpse of a monolithic structure shimmering and glimmering in the distance. The cubic structure isn't going anywhere, so the man keeps his pace. All is aglow in an assortment of brilliant colors. As he draws nearer, he distinguishes a number of people on and around the structure. Many are by themselves, while others are paired together. Most of the pairs are climbing the massive cube while the other individuals attempt to claw into or extract smaller cubes, from which the structure is seemingly constructed. So far, none of the smaller cubes appear to have been opened.

Most of the people are dirty, haggard, and starving, dressed in simple, coarse robes and not much else. In each pair, however, one figure is always sharper, slicker, and more sinister: demons with humans' faces, or humans with demons' faces, the man is uncertain.

The man stops to watch one pair arguing at the top edge of the cube. Swaying slightly. Sinking somewhat. The demi-human's voice is low, condescending:

"Have you no faith? We promised to deliver you from making the same mistakes over and over, living through the same agonies, and here we are. You are free, just as we said."

"But I'm *not*. I'm *not* free to leave. I've been stuck with you ever since. And I still have *these* welded to my palms." The short, skinny man in a purple cloak waves his arms and tries to open his fingers, but his grip won't loosen. One hand holds a jewel-encrusted golden scepter. The other: a long pair of silver tongs.

"But you're free to leave any time now. All you have to do is take your first step. Your faith will carry you wherever you wish to go and your obligation will be fulfilled."

"*And the price?* You still haven't named it?"

"We can discuss that later."

"That's what you keep saying: *always later*. What about –"

"Not to worry. Let us help you, then you can help us."

"But how will you find me?"

"Have no fears. We will. Now make your leap."

Resigned, the cloaked figure steps toward the edge and jumps forward. Momentarily, he is held in the air. All smiles, thinking he's a success, he quickly falls to the desert below where his spine is snapped and he is killed – but nowhere near instantly.

Cries out in agony: "YOU LIED!!"

The demi-human gazes down, unimpressed. "So much for your faith. It's not our fault. See you in the next realm."

The cloaked man is drawn downward into the dune long before anyone can even begin to care about his cries, until finally, he disappears; the scepter being the last to be sucked into the sand. His companion simply shrugs and vanishes to make room for the next pair. Aside from the man, no one pays much attention to this episode, but carries on with his or her own pursuits. As for the man, he has little sympathy for the cloaked figure.

He mutters: "He should have known better."

Closer, the man sees that all of the square surfaces are elaborately covered with a countless variety of glossy wrapping paper and cheap plastic ribbons and bows. Each cube is an individual cardboard box stacked and stapled, tied and taped to the others. Many have pieces of their paper, ribbons and bows torn off. The sand is littered with these bits. Each cube vying for attention, begging to be chosen. Unwrapped. Opened.

As the man passes by, he knocks on several of the cubes, remembering the back room of *Ye Olde Wonkey Shoppe*. And as before:

Empty.

Empty.

Empty.

Soon, another couple reaches the top. This time a woman makes the leap, but she immediately drops and dies on the dunes below. Her companion – demonic human or humane demon – quickly disappears as the sand swallows her whole.

Thus far, no one has paid the man any heed, nor does he wish to receive any attention. So, satisfied that this has nothing to do with The Emperor's domain, the man walks onward and he doesn't look back.

The next moment, however, the man is facing a demi-human. He stops. No. *Definitely a demon.* It appears to smile – all teeth – but its features are blurred, constantly shifting, or perhaps it has several faces. In the watery voice of many, it speaks:

"Leaving so soon? No desire to test your faith?"

The man's weathered face darkens; and although he is motionless, his whole being radiates pure rage. The demon stumbles backward, visibly afraid, but determined in its mission. It tries to compose itself.

" . . . ah, how about a gift then? Pick any one you like . . . any one at all . . . or more. Whatever you desire. Truly. That's what they're here for . . . Every box holds a special prize . . . Believe us."

The man remains silent. His fury grows with each second that passes and he takes a step towards the demon. His aura alone forces it backward, stumbling in extreme pain, but still it persists.

"Well then, how about – "

The man drops his small suitcase and thrusts his arm upward, his fingers knotting together. Even before he completes the gesture, the demon evaporates into a nauseous cloud of agony and fear. The desert heat quickly consumes the wisps of remaining vapor. Still seething with rage at being confronted in this way, the man takes up his suitcase and storms away. It's quite some time before he is calm again.

The wind dissipates and eventually dies. The man soon feels a great empathy with molded clay in a kiln but, like a piece of pottery, the man knows that if he makes it through this firing he'll be stronger than ever. *If* he makes it, being the key, of course. Seeing no change in the landscape, the man continues on his present course, hoping for the wind to rise again.

Sometime later, while scanning the horizon, the man spots what appears to be a stunted forest off to his left. Curious, he changes his direction and crosses the dunes toward the short woods. As he approaches, he soon realizes that they aren't stunted trees at all, but rather, they are crude crutches of all sizes driven into the sand. All are wooden, gnarled, brittle. Half-buried Ys baking in the sun. A cemetery of support. A grove of questions. Pointing. Divining. Simple splintered skeletal hands reaching outward. Reaching for him.

The man pauses outside their grasp. He can feel them straining. Yearning. Burning. Calling to him.

Consideration. They could possibly be useful, but it's not worth the risk. He's made it this far on his own. *How much farther can it be?*

Chuckling dryly, the man takes a wide berth around the grove and walks away, leaving the crutches whining and whistling behind him.

More time passes, but still there is no change in the heat, lighting or landscape. The man's pace finally begins to slow just as he approaches a rather large dune. Stopping for a moment, he closes his umbrella, intending to use it to help him climb the steep slope. Before he starts, he takes a deep breath and gathers his strength. Again, the man hesitates, but this time because he has caught someone's scent: stale sweat reeking through leather and denim. And something more. Something almost familiar, but he can't say what it is. Cautious, he takes his first steps and breathes as deeply as he can, noting any possible changes. As he ascends, he recognizes that *the someone* is male and most likely human. The man doesn't smell any fear.

On top, the man looks below to see the male figure, on his knees, repairing one of the towers for the massive sandcastle he is building. He's wearing a short leather jacket, a faded denim shirt, jeans, and runners. A white T-shirt is tied around his head and it's obscuring much of his bearded face. Nearby is an army surplus canvas shoulder bag. The bearded figure pauses and raises his right hand, waving briefly at the man.

"Hey."

The man pauses, then: "Hey."

Both remain in their places.

The male figure calls: "Come on down. It's no less cool down here, but at least we won't have to waste our energy shouting across to each other. You have nothing to fear . . . but I'm sure you already know that."

The man descends.

"I knew you were coming. I could feel your footsteps, then awhile later I caught a whiff of you, and – "

The man interrupts, standing above him: "Are you going to continue speaking through that T-shirt?"

"Oh, no. Sorry."

The bearded figure unties it and drapes it around his neck. He stands. Shakes off the sand. Then the two freeze as soon as they make eye contact. Although the younger man has much longer hair and a full beard, and despite the obvious age difference between the two – perhaps fifteen, twenty years or more – the resemblance is unmistakable: their lean physiques, their tanned, weathered faces, their steel gray eyes. The two continue to scan one another. Finally, the man breaks the silence.

"Who are you?"

"Just a man. You?"

"The same."

"You don't mean like *the same man* – like you're me when I get older?"

" . . . No . . . Well, not that I know of . . . I don't remember ever having a beard or such long hair. And you're a bit shorter than I am, but still . . . I've seen you before – "

"In dreams?"

The man nods.

"Me too. Especially lately." Pauses. Wonders aloud: "Uh, Dad?"

Grins. "I don't believe so?"

"But are you *sure*?"

"As sure as I can be."

"Then what's the deal? Are you even real or just some hallucination? Another dream? I've been in this desert for quite some time you know."

"I'm as real as you are; although I could be hallucinating or dreaming too, I imagine . . . I don't think I am, but I could be wrong, of course."

"Of course." Then, suddenly suspicious, the younger man takes a step back. "Are you a demon?"

"I suppose some may think so, metaphorically speaking, but really I'm just a man . . . If I were a demon though, I doubt I'd tell you the truth."

"So where does that leaves us?"

The man puts down his things. Sits on the sand. Faces the castle.

"I don't know. I wasn't exactly expecting to meet anyone out here at all . . . Not yet . . . I was just passing through on my way – "

"You're not here to tempt me?"

Raises an eyebrow. "Tempt you? No. Not at all. Why would I be here to tempt you?"

"Well, like I said, I've been here for quite awhile: six days and nights now – "

"Nights? You mean there are actually nights out here?"

"Sure." The younger man drops down beside him and sighs. Worn. Weary. "But I never know when they're going to happen. The day will go on and on and on. Always the heat . . . Always the silence . . . with only an occasional breeze as relief. The day will perpetuate itself until I can't take it any more, and just when I think it's going to end, it goes on. Then just before I've lost hope altogether, I'm cast into perpetual darkness and coldness and dampness – the exact opposite of how bright and hot and dry it is during the day. At first, it's a major relief, an ultimate lifesaver, but soon it becomes just as relentless and oppressive as it is during the daylight. And this cycle has continued for the last six days, but these days are extremely longer than how I know days and nights where I come from."

"But what are doing here in the first place?"

The younger man sighs even deeper. Then: "Me? I'm a prophet, if you can believe it. And I don't know if it's just the heat talking, but I have no idea who or what I'm supposed to be prophesying for, or what my message is supposed to be, either. Sometimes I even forget who I am. There's so much I don't know or understand."

"I see."

The prophet regards him seriously. "Do you? Do you really?"

Locking his eyes on the prophet, the man searches for a moment. Nods.

"Well then, for all I know, I could be prophesying your coming, and considering where I just came from, they could use a messiah. I tried to get them motivated . . . change things . . . even a little, but nobody was listening, and . . . to be honest, I'm really lousy at this. That's what I'm doing out here in the first place: putting in my forty days and forty nights, fasting, facing temptations – "

"And where have you been?"

The prophet gets up and goes back to repairing his sandcastle.

Squatting. "Oh, you know, here and there, in between . . . but most recently, I came from the obese tabby's domain."

The man nods slowly to himself.

The prophet continues: "I got pretty caught up in that whole scene for awhile – I still carry my misfortune with me." He reaches for his canvas satchel. "Would you like to – "

"No. No thank you. Not now."

He pauses, hands in the air. "It really has some rather innovative and frightening qualities. Buy now, pay later! Disaster to those who take their possessions for granted!"

The prophet shivers and shakes his head. Hard. Tries to lose the glow. Notices the man's curious look.

He explains: "A young woman told me that once. Well, actually she says that quite a lot."

The man bobs his head in understanding. "How is she?"

"As well as can be expected . . . She . . . She spoke of you often. She saw the similarities between us as well . . . something more . . . but it was pretty difficult to make out her babbling sometimes."

The man lets out a low whistle, elbows on his knees. Contemplative.

The prophet sits. Leans against his castle. Sand slides, towers topple, but the prophet no longer cares. Points at the man.

"You want a piece of advice: forget about what I said earlier. If you are some kind of messiah, *don't be*. It's not worth it. I'm a prophet, albeit a bad one, but I should know something about all this."

"Don't worry, I'm not a – "

"But that's a part of my job. At least I think it's a part of my job. Just like fasting and praying and having nightmarish visions and – "

"Building sand castles?"

The prophet glances back at his toppled structure. Shrugs. Crosses his arms.

"Well, other than any possible symbolic significance that comes to mind with building these things, I simply get bored. There's only so much fasting and praying and envisioning a prophet can do, you know. Sure, I record everything and that takes up a fair bit of time, but still . . ." He shivers again. Remembers some of the things he has seen. " . . . And then there are my temptations, but they only last so long. Sure, I get tempted every day, but – " Leans forward. Points. "Like someone comes along and says: turn a stone into a loaf of bread . . . Or: strike a stone to draw water . . . You know what I get when I strike a stone?"

The man barely shrugs.

"If I'm lucky I get sparks – but there's no kindling, let alone wood anywhere around here that I can find, so big fat hairy deal . . . But still, dangling before me: food, wine, water, women. Or how about making a leap of faith? Or worship me and all this will be yours . . . Would you like to own this desert?"

The man remains silent.

"Exactly . . . Or how about a way out of here?"

"Are you still speaking rhetorically?"

"Does it matter? The point is, I'm still here."

"Building sand castles."

"A prophet's gotta do what a prophet's gotta do."

The man stands. Dusts himself off.

"Well, I guess I don't really have anything to tempt you with."

He stops, considers the gum in his pocket and The Prize in his suitcase. Realizes that the prophet probably already has the power of The Prize, even if he can't remember it at the moment. As for the gum? Well . . .?

"Well, nothing you'd accept . . . and I don't have any of those other things you mentioned. I'm simply searching for a way out of here myself. You're welcome to – "

Snaps: "Oh you're a sly one, aren't you? You have *nothing*, except that I can go with you *IF* I want to. Why don't you try reverse psychology on me already – tell me I'm not welcome so I'll follow just to annoy you."

Undisturbed, the man takes up his suitcase and opens his umbrella.

"The choice is yours."

The prophet falls to the desert laughing maniacally.

"Yes! Of course! Of course it is!"

"Well, I have The Emperor to meet, I hope. Sorry I don't have anything for you, but like I said I don't imagine you'd accept it anyway."

Still laughing. Sparse tears rolling.

" . . . accept it anyway . . ."

" . . . and thanks for the advice."

" . . . vice . . ."

"I'll see you again."

With that, the man steps away, leaving the prophet rolling over his castle. Again and again and again. As the man crosses the next dune, he hears the prophet whisper:

"I'm afraid you probably will."

ONE HAND CLAP

Eventide. Rolling in. Rolling over. Crashing. Consuming. Drawing in. Drawing under. Taking away. Not leaving much behind.

As always.

The young woman wanders down the unlit alleyway, holding her misfortune close to her heart. Humming. She stumbles.

Stammers: "What am I doing? What am I doing? I don't know what I am doing . . . Where is everybody?! Don't you know: wherever you go, there you are?! Don't you know?! Don't know! Don't know! Don't go!! No . . . No no no."

She trips. Falls. Decides to stay awhile amongst the refuse, ignoring the stench. No one to stop her. Curls up. Rocking. Eventually rolls onto her back. Gazing upward, outward. Darkness in waves. Blanketing her in coldness. She sings, remembering the lyrics – one line at a time – that the prophet taught her a short time ago, before he left for the desert. As per usual, her voice is deadpan and badly off-key.

> "Go and sing for the birds and the trees.
> Try and stop/start? another disease.
> Take up whatever cause you please –
> But who will mourn for the dinosaur?
>
> Go and fill our skies with smog and death,
> Then try to . . . something something something"

She pauses, mumbling to herself. Concentrating. Thinks she has it right. Continues:

> "Then try to deny it with your shallow breath.
> Just take it all until there's nothing left –
> So who will mourn for the dinosaur?
>
> You can go out and get a gun –
> Then kill someone for a place in the sun.
> Or some will do it just for fun –

But who will mourn for the dinosaur?

Go and watch TV to forget your fears.
Leave your kids to be raised by their peers.
Everyone says they listen but nobody hears –
So who will mourn for the dinosaur?

Ignore the problems between white and black.
Hide behind your wealth for what you lack.
Dream we all go on so don't look back –
But who will mourn for the dinosaur?

So look to somewhere better than here –
Meanwhile watch each species disappear.
But remember that every wish hides a fear –
So who will mourn for the dinosaur?"

The young woman pauses again, swallowing what bit of saliva she has left to sooth her raw throat. Suddenly, she laughs – still not knowing what a tree or a dinosaur is – and she doesn't stop laughing for quite some time. With tears running down her grimy cheeks, she thinks of The Fray.

"Shades of gray." She whispers. "Shades of gray."

She remembers the man in the crowds before The Fray. Somehow she knew he was looking for her, but she didn't want him to see her again quite so soon. The young woman didn't know what to do then, either. Now she wishes that she had allowed herself to be seen. Perhaps he would have come up to her again. Perhaps he would have stayed. Or perhaps he would have taken her with him, wherever he went. Or perhaps . . .

Perhaps.

Perhaps.

Perhaps.

She snaps: "WHEREVER YOU GO, THERE YOU ARE!!!!"

Her words die almost immediately after their birth and there is no response from anyone or anything.

She stands. "DO YOU HEAR ME?!?!"

Grabbing her misfortune, she starts to run door to door, banging on them, even though there are no lights or other signs of life to be seen anywhere.

"Where are you?! Under the stars somewhere? I've heard about those too, you know, but I've never seen them myself. So where then? Under the stairs? Or the signs . . . time is rushing by and I don't know what to do . . . Where to begin? The start isn't always the best, you know."

She turns a corner but it is no less dark. Still, she cries out, waiting to be challenged. Wanting some answers, or an audience at the very least.

"Don't be deceived, dragged in . . . dragged down under. The stones are falling – can't you hear them? An avalanche . . . covering . . . collapse-relapse . . . perhaps . . . I can feel them, you know, placed upon me, pressing against me . . . Tell me a color and I'll try to move to it . . . Remove the stones and I'll try to move freely . . ."

She laughs maniacally and starts twirling down the middle of the street – kicking up garbage along the way – with no particular destination in mind. Still cackling, she cries:

"WELL, I GUESS I'VE BEGUN NOW, HAVEN'T I?!?!"

Arms wrapped around herself, spinning ever faster, she sings, creating her own melody as she goes along:

> "Carry me . . . Carry me through the portals –
> I can't make it alone. Too much time alone.
> Normally . . . normally I could make it
> But now is not the time to be alone."

Stirring in the shadows, but unseen by the young woman: Goons in waiting. Watching her. Waiting. Hungry, so hungry, but they have their orders. Waiting.

Waiting.

Losing her balance, the young woman spins out of control. Feet tripping on themselves, she sprawls on the asphalt, her misfortune flying from her grasp. Sucking in air, choking on her laughter, the woman waves her arms and legs up and down, out and in, forming a litter angel.

After the angel is complete, she springs up onto her knees and randomly points her fingers. The Goons' muscles tense, wondering if they have been discovered.

"What do you see? Hmmm? What do you see in the darkness? See, hmmm? See *him*? Or just a sea? Sea of what?" On her knees, she scans the shadows while more Goons move into place. Sniffing the air, she smiles slyly, happy to finally have an audience. "Here's the test, boys: how poetic can you get in your reply?"

Suddenly, the Goons rush forward from all sides. The woman springs towards her misfortune and clutches it protectively. No concern for her own well being; not thinking that she is actually their prey, and not her misfortune.

"Oh, I'm sorry. I forgot you boys don't even have mouths, let alone eyes."
She is surrounded. "So, perhaps I should rephrase my questions."

The Goons stop. They are all armed, as per usual, with an assortment of
pipes, blades, boards and bones, but no one touches her. One simply points
with his lead pipe the direction she is to go.

Somewhat surprised that she isn't already dead, the young woman chooses
to follow. As she takes a step, the Goons do the same. Holding her head high
and her misfortune close to her heart once again, she enjoys the "escort."

Soon after they are on their way, she decides to test and tease them a
little, *just because.*

"Are you willing to die?" She says to no one in particular, already knowing the answer. Then: "But are you willing to die for me?"

No response.

"Would you?" She points at one.

"Could you?" At another.

"Should – "

She stops for a moment, lost in her thoughts, but she is quickly – and
relatively gently – prodded forward.

Consideration. Then: "So have we reached the middle, boys? Or do you
know what I'm talking about? Did you get to hear my whole speech? It was
good one. Really. I began . . . and now . . . somewhere . . . well, in the street
obviously. Not in a mindfield . . . rarely on the beaten path . . . or the
straight road . . . or The Emperor's highway . . . or left in the ditch . . . left
like roadkill . . . left behind, left blind, to rot like the rest of humanity."

She stops. Snorts. Giggles. Spittle sprays.

"This is what I get for hanging out with a prophet for a couple of days.
Let me tell you – "

And she is prodded forward once more – not quite as gently as the first
time, either.

They weave through several side streets and alleyways, but the woman
soon realizes their eventual destination: *Ye Olde Wonkey Shoppe.*

"So where does that leave us, boys? Have the parameters been set? Are
they etched in stone? Would it matter if they were? Stones can be cracked.
Stones can be broken. Stones can be crushed: into gravel, into sand, in the
palm of – "

This time it is the Goons who stop dead in their tracks. They draw their
weapons. The young woman almost walks into one, but stops just in time.
She bobs and weaves trying to see who or what would make them halt so
abruptly.

A block away in the middle of the street, the figure stands. Although the figure is mostly lost in the shadows, the Goons immediately sense his tall, lanky form; his garments of soft gray leather; and most importantly, his extensive collection of tools. They feel him and know he sees them as well.

The figure remains unmoved while the Goons stand indecisively. They know only too well what happened to the first group of Goons the figure encountered. Despite that, all has been well between him and the others since his arrival. But still . . . *to let him go?* Surely, they could fare better than the others did, even though there was a score the first time and only half that number now. Surely –

The young woman decides for them.

"Hey, uh . . . carpenter – I know that's not your name or anything, but that's what you do isn't it? You building something tonight?"

The figure's eyes shine across the distance. The Goons' apprehension grows but they hold their ground. The young woman is left in the middle unable to break through.

"No, not tonight, Mistress."

"Just out for a walk then, like us?"

"Something like that."

"Would you care to join us then?"

"No. Thank you, but I believe we are heading in opposite directions this eventide."

The young woman reflects on this for a moment, then:

"Please say 'hello' to him for me when you see him."

The figure smiles. Nods. "And would you do the same for me? I'm not sure if or when I will return."

"I will."

And with that, the figure tips his hat and he is gone. Vanished.

The Goons still stand poised for more than a minute, their senses reaching, weapons ready, wondering if he will reappear on another side and attack them. There is no sign of the figure anywhere, however, and there is a collective, internal sigh from the Goons.

Meanwhile, the young woman also darts her eyes around, and occasionally she pokes at the some of the Goons. Finally she says, mocking them:

"Now what are guys so nervous about? He's not so bad."

The Goons say nothing in response – of course – and simply prod her along again. They cross over cautiously when they reach the area where the figure was standing only moments before. But he is clearly absent. They continue, and for the remainder of their journey, the young woman stays silent.

A short time later, they are standing before the door to *Ye Olde Wonkey Shoppe* and, as quickly as the Goons initially appeared, they are now gone.

Suddenly, standing there alone, the young woman no longer feels quite so confident.

"Wait! Don't go! Don't leave me! I need you! I – you want to know something funny, boys: I was wrong, there isn't a middle . . . and I'm not *always* going in circles!" She pauses, and speaks only for herself. Consoling: "I'm making progress – I could sure show that prophet a thing or two, anyway." She peers into the shadows. "What was I saying about progress?"

The young woman turns back to see the obese tabby sitting in the open doorway.

"Oh, never mind." She swallows, head down, avoiding the tabby's gaze.

"Greetings, Mistress." The cat purrs. "It's been quite some time."

" . . . yes . . . "

"You've been making quite a ruckus tonight, haven't you?"

" . . . yes . . . "

"Well, no real harm done . . . I applaud your efforts. Truly." The tabby grins, one paw in the air, welcoming her, as it leans against the door, holding it open. "Please come inside. There's much I'd like to discuss with you."

Somewhat fearfully, reluctantly, the young woman steps inside the shop. The front room – now lit softly by several candelabras – is still just as empty as she remembers it from her purchase in the past. Set out on the counter between the candelabras is a bottle of wine, some moldy slices of cheese, broken crackers, and a bowl of pungent herbs.

With a great effort, the obese tabby hops up onto a chair, then onto the counter, and scoops up a pawful of herbs. Breathing heavily after the sudden exertion, it soon munches.

Offers the bowl. "Catnip? Only the best, I assure you."

"No. Thank you."

Still breathing deeply, the tabby takes up another pawful. Its sapphire blue eyes are already beginning to glaze over. Shining in the warm light.

"Please, help yourself."

The young woman's stomach rumbles and she timidly crosses over to the counter. She remembers only too well her one and only purchase here – the last one ever made in the obese tabby's domain – and where it has led her. Despite her reservations, however, her hunger wins the argument. Tentatively, she sets her misfortune on the counter, takes up a piece of cheese and places it on a soda cracker. The young woman raises them to her lips and sniffs. She can't recall if the cheese is supposed to smell this badly or not.

The obese tabby tilts its head and waves its paw nonchalantly.

"Have no fears, Mistress. Only the best, remember? The cheese is supposed to look and smell that way. Quite a delicacy, I assure you. Besides, I have no interest in seeing you harmed. Poisoning is far too easy . . . in fact I find it rather *passé* . . . So, please."

Eyes wide, she takes a tiny nibble and chews carefully. She hadn't been concerned about being poisoned until the cat mentioned it just now. But so far, so . . . something . . . It's real food, at least, and it's considerably better than anything she's had to consume in a very long time.

The obese tabby grins, happy to be a successful host once more. It has another pawful of catnip, then pours out two glasses of red wine. Handing one to the young woman, it proposes a toast. Holding its glass out with both paws, the cat raises its voice.

"To my Nemesis: may I never find another more worthy."

No less hesitantly, the woman clinks her glass against the tabby's. She slowly sips it while the obese tabby knocks back half of its glass. At least the wine tastes better than the cheese and cracker. Her throat warms immediately as she swallows, and she sips a little more to maintain the burning sensation.

Refilling its glass, the tabby begins: "Now that the festivities have begun and we have broken bread together, so to speak, shall we attend to business?"

Eyes wide. *"Business? With me?"*

"But, of course, Mistress. You're very special, don't you know that?"

Scowling. "That's what I keep hearing, and I must say I'm getting a little tired of it already."

"My apologies then." The obese tabby has another mouthful of wine, then takes up another pawful of catnip. Munches contentedly. Then: "But I only mention it because the time is coming for people to see just how special you really are."

"Special?!" She snorts. Rants, spittle flying: "I know absolutely nothing about being special! No memory of . . . of . . . No feelings – except for the pain of responsibility. No time – everything is moving so fast, I can't keep up. No control over what I need. No life – to be wasted . . . Wasted! No death – but still, it seems like I'm living on borrowed time. No happiness–" She pauses. Tears in her eyes. "– just kidding."

The obese tabby puts down its glass of wine and reaches out to her.

"Come here, please. Scratch me behind the ears and I'll do the same for you. I'll help you, Mistress . . . but I really need you to help me even more."

"But how can *I* help *you*?" The young woman sniffs, then wipes under her nose with the sleeve of her coat.

"Let me explain."

She hesitates, but eventually she crosses over to the obese tabby and does as it asks. The cat leans against her and begins to purr almost immediately. It's quite some time before they leave the old store.

DRIVE THE TEXTURED SKY

Twilight. Bruised. Bloodied. Twilight. Glossy. Chilly. Twilight. Alive! But with a little death here and there, of course. As always. Twilight.

The figure stands alone in the street. Considers his options. He has been waiting— much longer than he had originally anticipated, to be sure. But not time wasted. No. He's been gathering what he needs; although he has to admit he would much rather have confronted the man long before now. Have him . . . *things* . . . taken care of properly. However, he won't change anything, nor will he underestimate the man again. And neither will he wait for him any longer.

Time to go.

But which way?

Try and follow the man's trail leading away from The Garden of Earthly Delights and into the mountains? Or take a short cut through The House of Mirrors? Or in The Funhouse? Or is it time to take flight and create a portal of his own— head him off before the man can do anything more?

The figure wonders, hands on his hips, long fingers of his right hand softly caressing the cold steel of his pump action nail puller. *Why the indecision?* That question alone has kept him up late too many times since his arrival here. But no longer.

Time to go.

The figure searches the sky— always overcast, at least since he's been here. Clouds rolling, swirling, crashing together. Sometimes silent, but never still. Sometimes transforming into one, but at what cost?

Sighing, the figure stands, lost in the battle above. Making mental notes. Calculating the odds for various outcomes. Learning all the while. Watching. Waiting.

A short time later, the figure is drawn back down to the street, hearing the approach of many. Counting the footfalls, he hears the voice of the young woman. He remains where he is, relaxed, hands still resting on his hips. Waiting.

Eventually, the Goons with the young woman in their midst round the corner one block away, and they stop immediately, suddenly sensing his presence. He smiles inwardly, quite satisfied with the Goons' fear and apprehension, especially in contrast to the young woman's naive curiosity. The figure sees her rising on her toes and taking small hops to see why they have stopped.

There is no challenge here, even though he can sense the internal debating amongst the Goons. He knows they have another mission concerning the young woman, and he won't dispatch them unless they absolutely force him to do so.

Not too surprisingly, it's the young woman who speaks out after finally seeing with whom they are dealing. The figure can't help but smile at her audacity. Eyes shining, he feels the growing anxiety of the Goons, wondering when they will finally lose control and rush him. He does his best to keep his voice equable in his replies, attempting to calm the fears of the Goons. No need to frighten the young woman or upset the obese tabby in laying them to waste unnecessarily.

The figure soon realizes that, given the chance, she would keep him hear talking all night, or at least until the Goons finally couldn't take it any more. He decides it is time to go.

"I believe we are heading in opposite directions this eventide."

The figure marks her hesitation, her consideration, and he's further surprised at her astuteness:

"Please say 'hello' to him for me when you see him."

He understands more than ever the obese tabby's great interest in her. The figure smiles for her to see.

Nodding at her. "And would you do the same for me? I'm not sure if or when I will return."

"I will."

And with that, the figure tips his hat and he is gone. He decides to create his own portal after all and then cut over to The House of Mirrors. As he vanishes, drawing away, he can feel the collective sigh of the Goons and hear the young woman's playful rebuking. Chuckling, he propels upward, outward, moving through one mass to another— soon ending up outside the entrance to the Mirror House.

Not wanting to cause any unwanted attention by his sudden appearance, the figure quickly steps inside the brilliantly lit entrance before he is seen. The light is reflected off of the floor, walls, and ceiling which are all covered with brightly polished mirrors. The figure eases his way through, winding through various corridors; carefully choosing which branch to take each time; ascending and descending onto various levels. All the while his image is reflected continuously in countless ways.

Sometimes, he really has to laugh, and he does so without caring who might overhear him. Sometimes, he pauses, not because he is uncertain about which way to go, but because his reflection draws him in. Sometimes, the light is captured just right and he becomes mesmerized, finding it difficult to move onward. His face isn't so rugged, his scars disappear, his flesh is fuller, more alive, and he sees a joy in his eyes that he can barely remember possessing once. And all he can see is *himself*.

Each time he stops, however, he is eventually able to break free, but finds it increasingly difficult to move onward. Thus, despite the maze being surprisingly easy, the figure soon discovers he would much rather stay than attempt to locate the exit.

In several of the corridors, the figure finds many others who are in similar predicaments: held immobile, hypnotized by their own reflections, or caressing themselves or their images, licking the surfaces repeatedly, finding the perfect poses. Most still carry their misfortunes close to their hearts, while others have actually been able to part with them; although, these circumstances are no better, of course. Many are near death from starvation and dehydration, never appearing to have moved in weeks or more. The stench of death and decay is everywhere.

The figure does his best to avoid getting too close to anyone, as much for keeping them away from his reflection as to keep out of theirs. No one notices him pass by, and that suits him fine in his new quest for the ultimate reflection of himself *for himself*.

Soon, he begins to move more frantically through the maze, searching desperately, knocking aside the barely living and stepping on the dead. Until, he rounds a corner and finds *the spot*, or so he believes from where he is standing. Moving closer could change things. Perhaps. Besides, there is already someone standing there, transfixed. Yes. Standing in *his* place is the old misfortune teller— dressed as loudly as usual in her billowing blouse, patchwork skirt and a kerchief tied over her head. But she is more dirty and haggard than ever before.

The old woman catches a glimpse of him in the corner of her varicose eyes. Fearful but resolute, she digs in her heels. Soles squeak. Smudge the surface. She calls over her shoulder, not wanting to part with her reflection, despite the great danger she feels in the possibility of losing her place. There is *nothing* worth leaving it for.

She begins: "All is not as—"

Without thinking, the figure's right hand blurs and brushes lightly against his chest. A circular saw blade flies from his fingers and rips through the throat of the haggard old woman. Thin, tired blood splatters across the mirrors, further destroying the potentiality of his perfect reflection; while surprisingly, the blade bounces off of the surface. It's reflected off the surrounding walls several times until it ends up spinning and wobbling on the floor by the old woman's feet. There's not a scratch on any mirror.

As her body drops to the mirrored floor, the figure rushes forward. He whips out his crowbar and snaps the hooked end under her neck, breaking her fall and also several vertebrae. Dipping down, he uses his whole body and tosses her around the next bend. The walls and floor shake, but again, no mirrors break. This is not the first time someone has been murdered for a prime position. And what the unbroken mirrors say about his luck, the figure is uncertain. Nor does he really want to know. No.

The figure returns to his prime position. As quickly as his tools were drawn, they are now cleaned and replaced. Resting.

Or *restless?*

Waiting for more?

Undoubtedly.

But now, standing here, watching the blood trail down the reflective walls, the image, while actually enhanced, is not the same any more. The figure is not the same. To be sure, he never is, but now he sees himself *as himself* once more. Briefly, he darts his eyes around and contorts his body in a variety of ways, still attempting to find "perfection" again. But the moment passes and he accepts what he sees.

"Am I so weak?" He barely utters. Trembles. Shakes. Holds back his tears. Takes off his battered Stetson and wipes his bald pate with a kerchief from his back pocket. Wonders about how he was so easily overcome. Wonders if the woman's sometime companion, the large snake, is anywhere nearby, and if so, will it seek vengeance? Further wonders if the man had been tempted in such a way, and if so, how did he fare? What to do? What to do?

Soon, however, the figure is past wondering— he has more pressing matters to deal with now. Ultimately, he's glad he's alone and no one witnessed this sorry event. He takes out his art and balances it on his right index finger. All is . . . as it is. So, once again:

Time to go.

As he passes the old woman, he hesitates for a minute, memorizing her resting-place and how she died— attempting to give her death some meaning.

He addresses her corpse— his voice low and even:

"If I had not taken your life, I would still be standing there or somewhere else in this maze, until I would be lying there just like you . . . Thank you."

He pauses, replacing his hat. Then: "It is impossible to achieve the end without suffering."

With that, he is gone through the last twists and turns. He feels his way along. Eyes closed. His other senses reaching. No need to take further risks. Besides, he has had enough of himself for the time being.

No one else crosses his path and eventually he is out the exit. He opens his eyes to find himself in an abandoned gift shop. Gray light filters in through the dirty windows. The dust is thick on the countless pewter framed hand mirrors, T-shirts, sweatshirts, postcards, key chains, and more — all proclaiming lines such as:

"WHAT LIES
UNDER
YOUR SKIN?"

And:

"I JUST REALIZED
THE DEPTH
OF MY OWN
SHALLOWNESS."

And:

"I SAW MYSELF FOR THE FIRST TIME AND
I LIVED TO BUY THIS LOUSY T-SHIRT."

The figure casually walks through the store, somewhat curious but, more importantly, he is searching for signs of the man's passing. All of the items are from a first edition line, and it doesn't take him long to realize that *no one* before him has ever made it through The House of Mirrors; not alive, anyway.

The figure takes up a Mirror House piggy bank, which is a small replica of the original maze, then pulls off one of the top buttons from his shirt and spins it through the "ENTRANCE" slot. He hears it roll and rebound off of the tiny walls. Occasionally he catches a glimpse in the multiple mirrored surfaces, but he is careful not to get trapped looking too long inside the maze.

After a minute, however, the figure is not surprised to see the button is lost in its depths, rather than making its way to the exit. He gives the piggy bank maze a shake and hears the button move a little more, but he can no longer see it. Suddenly, wanting his button, he draws his arm back and, with all of his strength, he throws the piggy bank against a nearby paneled wall.

The mini-Mirror House does not shatter, but rather, it goes through the thick wall. Large splinters fly and the piggy bank maze lands outside. The figure hears it bouncing on the rocks, but still he doesn't hear the breaking of glass. Enraged, the figure storms for the door and grabs a couple of T-shirts along the way, which he stuffs into his leather pack.

Outside, he stands on a vast, rocky plateau, with the wind whipping around him. A short distance away, a sky trolley shack sits, equally abandoned, with cables trailing down the sparsely wooded mountainside. Cobbled paths lead through the rough terrain to the gift shop and directly behind it to a grand resort hotel, and elsewhere along the plateau.

The figure cares nothing for the buildings or for the potential treasures and mysteries that might be inside. His only wish is to retrieve his button and leave this place. Too much time wasted wandering and wondering.

He soon spots the intact piggy bank maze resting amongst the rocks, unscratched. Inside, his button remains hidden, locked away. *Was there a key for the bank back in the gift shop?* The figure rotates the replica in his hands but finds no keyhole. Only his furious features are reflected back at him, in an infinite number of ways, none of which attract him at all. And on the opposite side of the "ENTRANCE," there is only a single narrow opening with the tiny word "EXIT" carved into the surface above it. Mocking him.

Holding the mini-Mirror House in his hands, his fingers tense and he considers crushing it into dust. Without holding anything back he knows he can do it. The figure increases the pressure and finally feels the Mirror House maze giving way. The sharp corners cut into his hands, but he ignores the pain and the damage done. Then suddenly he stops himself. Here is a challenge. A puzzle: one in which he failed on a much larger scale only minutes before. One now that he could end with simple brute force, but what would he gain, really?

The figure relaxes and he gives the piggy bank maze a swift shake. Yes. He hears the button rattling inside. He takes out the T-shirts. With one, he quickly wraps the replica, not out of fear of it breaking, but because it could cut him again when he might least expect it. With the other, he wipes his hands, which are already beginning to heal; although they will now boast new scars, of course.

Satisfied, the figure steps away and crosses towards the edge of the plateau. Standing by the short stone fence, the figure searches the overcast sky, the rocky landscape, and draws a dry smile across his cracked, brown, hourglass teeth. The man is near and he will find him, *soon*, and then . . .

"And then we shall see . . ."

IN THE COURT OF THE CRIMSON EY'D KING

Post meridian. Post-modern? Well, perhaps leave that for the crickets to decide— chirruping in the tall, dry grass of this small treeless oasis; seeing nothing but more and more dull gray and green; hearing nothing but their own voices.

The man walks slowly, each step an effort. His small suitcase is in one hand; his umbrella is in the other, shielding him somewhat from the extremely intense desert heat. The white chalk X on the suitcase's side mostly faded away. Forgotten.

Ahead of him, a massive cast iron double gate stands. There is no fence stretching out on either side, nonetheless, the man decides to pass *between*— especially after he sees the inscription carved into a plate over the gate, which states:

FATUM FORTUNA CASUS

The man licks his cracked lips and laughs dryly.

"At least it's in the appropriate tongue."

Standing within arm's length of the double gate, he puts down his suitcase and closes his umbrella, placing it between the suitcase's handles. The man consults his works for a few moments and considers his options. Then, satisfied with what he sees, and happy that his works is almost fully recovered— although it will always be scarred— he pockets it and releases the gates' latch. There is some resistance and the latch squeals its protest as it is lifted. Straining his exhausted body, he pulls on both gates. The rusty hinges scream in ultimate agony, but eventually, they do open for him.

Under the arch, he kneels and rummages in a coat pocket. He pulls at the grass with his other hand, then digs in the coarse, dry sand creating a hole almost the size of his fist. Next, the man places the three seeds from his left hand in the hole, then knots the fingers in his right. Joints pop and bones crack while he recites a quick, but almost incomprehensible incantation. Squeezing his gnarled fist, the wound in his palm reopens and a single drop of clear fluid falls upon the seeds. Immediately, the seeds tremble with awakening and the man quickly covers them with the sand.

The man sighs. Trembles. Gradually stands. Whispers in consolation:

"It is impossible to achieve the end without suffering."

Drawing in a deep breath, he quickly thrusts his gnarled and broken fingers apart, resetting them. The wound in his palm remains open and his hand aches; he is too weak for it to begin healing quickly on its own. After binding his palm with a handkerchief, he gently flexes his fingers, making sure his fingers still work and the handkerchief will stay in place. Then, with an effort, the man takes up his suitcase and he passes through the open gates, leaving the seeds to do their part. The man doesn't bother to close the gates behind him.

On the other side, the grass has grown and it's still growing; evolving. Not very far away, tropical trees and shrubs stand. Flowers bloom. Birds chirp and call. Everywhere life is flourishing.

Using his umbrella before him, the man makes his own narrow path through the dense foliage, his destination in sight: a stone palace with towers reaching high above the tree line. The humidity is smothering, especially considering the arid, almost endless desert from which he has just arrived. However, the man still doesn't take off his long coat. He only unfastens another button on his shirt. It's not too far to go, at least by his sight.

Two hours later, the man finally reaches a clearing with the outer palace wall before him. Scaffolding has been erected fifty feet high around the entire wall. Tools are scattered on the scaffolding and on the ground. Despite it only being the late afternoon, no one is at work.

Thinly coated with whatever sweat he has left, the man makes himself presentable: tucking in and buttoning his shirt, knotting his tie, combing his hair, and so on. As satisfied as he can be given the circumstances, he crosses the clearing.

Drawing closer, he sees that the walls are completely covered in archaic writings and hieroglyphics from a variety of cultures. He recognizes many of the symbols: poets, prophets, politicians, and other people of power have all had a hand in carving these surfaces. Throughout, however, the walls are cracking and crumbling; the history eroding, falling apart.

From inside the palace walls, he can hear singing, joyful crying and orchestral music filling the air. Uttering a low whistle, the man walks over to the portcullis. Seeing no one in the open, he calls out hoarsely and waits to be challenged.

After more than a minute no one has appeared and the man calls out again, louder this time. But still the courtyard remains deserted. Many minutes and several shouts later, a guard arrives at a leisurely, slightly drunken pace. Bobbing along, he eyes the man from head to toe and back again, taking in the man's worn and weathered appearance and apparel. Uncertain.

Curious, but cautious. Hand on the pommel of his sword: resting lightly, but ready. Well, as ready as can be expected considering his intoxication.

" . . . Hmmm . . . uh, good day to you . . . sir."

The man nods. Sharpens his focus. "And to you."

"You have business—?"

"Yes. I'm here to see The Emperor. I believe I'm expected."

"Is that so?" The guard is still bouncing slightly up and down on the balls of his feet in no particular rhythm. "Have you . . . hmmm . . . a letter of introduction, or perhaps—?"

"No. Nothing really. I'm new around here."

Although he was initially unsure, the man also notices the guard's voice is out of sync with his whole face. He glances down briefly, checking for subtitles, but finds none.

"I see. Well then, I'm not so sure, unless perhaps you might . . . hmmm . . .?" The guard shakily draws up his hand and rubs the first two fingers against his thumb. " . . . hmmm . . .?"

The man smirks, reaching for his works, desiring to end this quickly and move onward. He reconsiders, wishing to maintain some anonymity, for the time being at least. So instead, he reaches into another vest pocket and tosses a pop bottle cap to the guard, who almost misses it. The guard recovers and springs back erect, but quivering. He eyes the old cap carefully, almost bites it just to be sure, but stops himself just in time. Turning it in his fingers, he lets out a low, appreciative whistle. Finally, he pockets it and steps back.

"Just a moment, sir, while I raise the . . . uh, port-ih-cull-ihs."

Inside the courtyard, the portcullis lowered again behind the man, the guard leads him to the main hall. The guard continues to bob with each step, his arms stretched out and waving.

Relaxing his vision, the man finally catches a glimpse of the fine lines attached to the guard's joints. He searches above, but soon loses sight of the almost invisible strings. Curious, but not terribly concerned for the moment, the man decides to open up on another topic of interest for him.

"I noticed the scaffolding outside—"

Snorts. "Hard to miss 'em . . ." Quickly realizes his impropriety. "Uh, my apologies, sir."

"No offense taken. Go on, tell me."

"Well, uh, it's been there for as long as I can remember. The Emperor has people trying to restore all that stuff on the outer walls practically everyday, working their way around the palace. But, by the time they get back to where they first began, they uh, have to start all over again. It's very frustrating. So much is lost . . . So much that can't be saved in time . . . hmmm . . .

Other writings become changed and distorted— sometimes by accident . . . sometimes on purpose. Simply too many elements against it. But The Emperor wants it preserved as best as it can be, so it is done . . . in a manner of speaking."

"And today?"

" . . . hmmm? Well today is The Emperor's birthday, of course, so everyone is inside celebrating. I just uh, happened to come outside for some air and cool off a bit. Otherwise, you may have been calling out there until tomorrow afternoon . . . or uh, even longer . . . hmmm."

The two pass the main doors but the man doesn't object. They walk around the corner to another smaller door and the guard stops there, wobbling. Strings shining occasionally.

"Now just follow me inside, hmmm. After we're in the hall, you're on your own, not unless you happen to have another one of—"

"This will be fine."

The guard nods, a little angry with himself for not getting more from the man. However, he doesn't attempt any betrayal, or subterfuge, not knowing what the man is capable of and not being in prime fighting condition, even when he is sober.

They pass through several corridors— the strings never slackening. Unlike the obese tabby's domain, The Emperor's palace is clean and in a much better state of repair. Tapestries depicting several of The Emperor's early conquests in other domains adorn the walls, which are interspersed with brass sconces. Music, singing and laughter grow louder and more cacophonous with each step. The fragrance of flowers, herbs, roasted meats, vegetables, and pastries waft through the air, along with the smooth sweet scent of hundreds of beeswax candles. The man's stomach rumbles in anticipation.

Not wanting to be associated with the man just in case he causes any trouble, the guard mixes in almost immediately, but the man doesn't mind. He is happy to be on his own to observe for a moment.

The main hall is filled to capacity with people, dressed in a variety of styles and revealing a wide range of wealth: from T-shirts and jeans to tuxedos and ball gowns. Tea dresses, sun-dresses, leather miniskirts and tube tops. Shorts and sandals for some, robes and bare feet for others. Suits of every cut and uniforms from every service. Satin and silk, lace and leather, velvet and velour, polyester and body paint. From no make-up to clown make-up and every point in between. Gems and jewelry shine like a sea of tiny stars.

An orchestra plays to one side, and the man recognizes the three pale, but beautiful cellists from the Three-Ring Circus mixed in with the other musicians. Men and women. Young and old. Some traditional instruments: strings mostly, some flutes, oboes and recorders, several grand pianos, and tympani thundering in the background. Mixed in are an army of guitars, acoustic and electric, and two young men scratching vinyl. Listening for a moment, the man distinguishes five separate songs all being performed simultaneously by various sub-groups, usually at odds with one another, except at key moments where there is a perfect synthesis. No one seems to mind regardless of what is played. Hundreds of courtiers twirl and leap on the dance floor, while others shout and try to sing along, and fill their faces from the massive banquet tables.

Turning his head about the hall, the man sees everyone wobbling like the guard, even when they are supposedly standing still. Joints like loose springs constantly in motion. Voices too, all disconnected, discordant. Briefly, he scans the elaborately painted ceiling— which depicts the vast life around a coral reef in almost three-dimensional detail— but the fine lines are lost.

The man considers imitating the courtiers' actions, but only for a moment; he is far too drained to put out the effort. Nor does he care all that much. Instead, he does his best to tune out the raucous masses while his eyes grow tired from the perpetually chaotic motion. Fortunately, he doesn't stand out too much—well, except for his relative stillness and:

"Hey man, what's with the suitcase?" A reveler drunkenly points at him.

Others look. Heads bob and weave.

Another gestures at his umbrella: "It's not raining in here."

Some stare unsteadily. Then another courtier— also taking in the suitcase with the faint remnants of the white chalk X— shrieks:

"BOMB!!!!!"

The music stops. People scream. Some flee in terror. Meanwhile, many people ask:

"What's a bomb?!"

The crowd clears a circle around him as The Emperor's guards rush in towards him, fully armored, swords drawn. Wobbling. Although, once in actual sight of him, they come no closer than anyone else does. Waves ripple.

Over the din of the throng, the Captain of the Guard barks at him, his lips moving at a different speed in another tongue:

"Alright, what's in the suitcase?"

The man is unmoved. "Some clothes, toiletries, a couple of books, The Prize."

Silence engulfs the screams.

Several people faint.

The circumference of the circle extends another ten feet.

Lines tangle. Lots of lines.

Still, the man is unmoved.

Momentarily confused, the Captain of the Guard is uncertain if he should take the man at his word or not. The decision is made for him. A low, melodious voice calls out:

"Clear the way. Let the man pass and approach me."

Immediately, a path for the man is opened, leading to the throne where The Emperor is seated. Guards line the way, all poised and ready, quivering— their revels forgotten. The man walks carefully, not wishing to alarm anyone and cause any unnecessary violence. Before the throne at the bottom of the stairs is a deep pool, with several tunnels leading away from it. The man notices the pool is empty at the moment and he passes it by without comment.

Naked, except for a pair of black sunglasses, The Emperor, a massive albino penguin, patiently waits. After all of the constant movement, the man is happy to see that The Emperor is unattached. Still. Calm. Regal. Well, relatively speaking— as regal as a huge penguin can be, anyway.

The man pauses at the foot of the marble stairs leading up to the throne. He puts his small suitcase on the raised ledge of the pool, with his umbrella between the handles, then bows slightly. The Emperor nods in satisfaction. After covering his mouth and clearing his parched throat, the man begins:

"It's a pleasure and an honor to finally meet you, your—"

"Call me Bernie."

" . . . Pardon me?"

"You heard me. You were going to call me *Your Highness?*"

"Yes."

"Or *Your Majesty?*"

"I—"

"Or *Your Majestical Highfulness?*" Pauses. "Well don't . . . Don't get all formal and hoighty-toighty pish-posh on me."

"But I—"

"Or what? *The Penguin?* Do I look like a comic book super villain, or even a super hero to you?"

The man remains silent. This is not exactly what he had expected. Well, the penguin, yes, but not all of this rigmarole. He also had intended to speak to The Emperor privately, not in front of The Emperor's entire Court. And considering the room full of sycophants, the man is greatly confused by The Emperor's request.

"I hate all these mish-mash titles and ehwhatnots. And since I am The

Emperor, I say call me Bernie."

"As you wish . . ."

"Bernie."

" . . . Bernie."

"And what's your name?"

The man swallows. Hard. Sweats the last bit of moisture out of him. The Emperor leans back, wings wide on the arms of his throne. Tilts his head. Pointing.

"Now don't tell me you simply go around being called *The Man*? Or just as *he, him, sir, that guy in the suit*? Or is it just plain *Suit*?"

"Well, I—"

"Your life is not an allegory, *man*. You *are* living it— however others may see it or interpret it— *but you are living it*. Give yourself some credit, *man*, some recognition. I'm an individual. Aren't you?"

"Certainly, I—"

"Well then?"

Glances around the hall. "It's just that . . . I've never really been asked before."

"Makes your shorts kinda squishy-wishy, doesn't it?"

" . . . You could say that."

"Well then?"

The man darts his eyes around, taking in The Emperor's retainers, musicians, guards, servants, Ladies and Gentlemen of the Court. Once again, he clears his throat, but finds himself unable to utter his name.

The Emperor shakes his head, somewhat sadly.

"Your reputation does not precede you, in regards to this matter, at least."

"My apologies . . . Bernie."

"Shall I clear my Court? Or even then, would you be afraid of spies hiding behind an arras or a mirror, or some other ehwhatnot waiting to discover your ever-so-secret name?"

The man holds his head high, and eyes locked on The Emperor, he announces his name to the Court. Upon hearing it, several more people faint, four have heart attacks and two have brain embolisms and all six die on the spot. Many others flee in absolute terror. Those that are a little worldlier simply step back and reach for the reassuring touch of another, or more commonly, for whatever stimulant they have on hand. The guards tighten their grip on their weapons. Some reach for talismans and relics. Still others barely acknowledge the freshly made wet spots on their groins.

Lines tangle like never before. Terrified and ignorant, bleating and babbling, bobbing and slobbering, the people make matters worse with each second that passes. Flushed, The Emperor nods at his guards, who clear the Court of the living, dead, and otherwise as quickly as they can. The body count grows substantially. The man holds his place and says nothing. Waiting.

After he is alone with the man, The Emperor speaks:

"Ooops . . . Oh well, my mistake. I understand why you keep that to yourself now. Sorry to have pushed you— just a little teasing, a little testing— but more importantly, I have to know with whom I am dealing."

"Understandable. But still, my apologies for disrupting your Court." The man bows slightly again. "I had no intention—"

"Tush-tush. Think nothing of it. It was all my fault. Besides, they need a really good scare once in a while. Unfortunately, or *fortunately*, as the case may be— this news will spread faster than . . . than . . . oh crap! Just when I thought I had a really great metaphor. Don't you just hate that? Well, anyway, let me just say it will be *fast*."

"I am no longer terribly concerned."

"Good."

The Emperor slides off his throne and waddles down the stairs. He leads the man to an antechamber filled with brightly colored plush pillows, embroidered with scenes from various holiday retreats— mostly tropical destinations. As well, there are several small tables covered with various fruits, dainties, and flagons of wine and water.

Propping himself up and getting comfortable, The Emperor gestures for the man to relax and do the same. The man does so, removing both his overcoat and his suit jacket, as well as his shoes. He drapes his coats over his suitcase, loosens the knot of his tie and sits at a respectable distance, not wanting to offend The Emperor, being very aware of his body odor after such a long journey.

The Emperor regards him for a moment. Then:

"Please, remove your tie and vest if you wish. Even your socks. Or more. Be as comfortable as you wish. As you see, I go around naked, except for my sunglasses, all the time. Remember: no formalities here, especially with just the two of us, or three of us, if you care to include your works."

The man nods, then removes his socks, tie, and vest, which he also drapes over his suitcase. His works remains in its home. He untucks his shirt and unfastens a few more buttons, but won't go further. Despite The Emperor's offer, it has been too long since he has been so informal in such a setting. Nonetheless, he is quite relieved to have removed these things, so he can rest a little more comfortably.

Satisfied that the man has settled in, The Emperor takes up a chocolate eclair between the ends of his wings and begins to nibble at it. The man gazes at him, bemused. The Emperor returns his gaze, grinning.

"How else do you think I keep my weight up? Krill? Shrimp? Fish? Ehwhatnot?"

The man simply smiles, pours himself some water, and tears open a pomegranate.

"Well I hate raw seafood. Detest it. It might not be so bad, if my first memories of it weren't digging it half-digested out of my father's gullet." As if to demonstrate, The Emperor starts pecking and sucking the whipped cream and custard out of the center. "And *ice*? Let me tell you . . . do you what it's like to be a penguin? What they do? How they spend their *entire lives*?"

Popping a single seed into his mouth, savoring the sweetness, the drop of moisture, the man shakes his head.

"We're born in an entirely hostile environment, with little to no protection from the elements. We eat if our mothers happen to return in time to feed our fathers, who have been starving to death keeping us warm in our eggy-weggies, then hatching us. Barely fed, we move onward, waddling across the frozen tundra, and to what? A watery mass wavy-grave; only to sink or swim; only to reproduce, and start the cycle all over again. Living to work . . . not to play . . . but to simply survive . . . not for fun, or for knowledge, or for any kind of noble advancement or other worthy-worldly ehwhatnots, but to simply hold off death for as long as we can. And the insane part is that generation after generation nobody has got any wiser. Everybody's doing the same thingy-wingy, just like they were doing it a millennia and more ago."

The Emperor tosses his sunglasses aside.

"Even me. Look at my funny-bunny eyes, my lanky white body. Well, it may not look all that lanky, but I'm pretty skinny for a penguin my size. You might think I had it a bit easier, but I didn't. Most wanted me to suffer right along with them and those that didn't simply wanted me dead, just for being different . . . for being *weaker*. Well, I showed them! Well, uh . . . actually I showed them nothing. They all think I'm long dead. Sure I'd like to gloat over them sometimes, but it's not worth all the bother just to bring them here for that. And I'm certainly never going back."

"But how did you end up here?"

The man takes a tiny sip of water, swishing it around before slowly swallowing it. Even then it goes down hard, like swallowing a razor blade. He replaces the goblet, wanting to wait for the trickle to settle for awhile before attempting another one.

"Like you, I simply found an opening and took advantage of it. And luckily things are different here. They've always been different too, but I arrived at a time of transition and it was fairly easy to get established. I must admit, that the survival instincts bred into me for generations have been a great benefit over these many, many years. I'm The Emperor, what else can I say?"

"What of your dealings with the obese tabby?"

"Ah, your Nemesis . . . As a mafia kingpin he has done very well for himself indeed, as I'm sure you know very well. However, since your arrival, well . . . you have really stirred things up; especially with your works' victory in The Fray, and after leaving the pyramid behind. And now that word of your true name will spread, who is to say what will happen next?" The Emperor pauses for a moment, regarding the man. "Let us be honest: what do you have to say on the matter? Why have you come? Not simply to pay me tribute on my birthday, I'm sure."

"With all due respect, no." The man hesitates, considering where he should begin. Then: "For all the time the obese tabby has been my Nemesis, we have never met. Our dealings . . . our confrontations . . . have always been at a distance. Neither of us had even crossed over to each other's realm until I arrived a short time ago, and that was simply by . . . chance . . ." The man pops another seed in his mouth. " . . . perhaps . . ."

"By Fate? No, you don't fool me. I can tell, you don't believe in Fate any more than I do." The eclair finished, The Emperor pours himself some wine and burrows further into the pillows. "A little test of your own? Well, let me tell you, this Emperor will not be led around—"

"What of the gate in the desert then?"

"Oh, that was constructed long before I ever arrived. I appreciated the nostalgia of it, even the irony perhaps. Besides, there's more than Fate being proclaimed there—"

"True enough."

"— and I saw no reason to remove or replace it. You liked it too, didn't you?"

"Certainly."

"But we are becoming distracted. You were just saying—"

"Yes. Well, I learned of an entrance to his realm, which was only recently uncovered, and I made a few arrangements. Then I came as quickly as I could before anyone else of importance decided to outflank me."

"So others know?"

"A few, but most have no true comprehension, and they have too much fear which will keep them away as long as I'm here."

The Emperor sips at his wine, savoring it— cleansing his pallet of the chocolate and whipped cream.

"So it's simply between you and the obese tabby then?"

"I imagine so."

"Show me."

Understanding, the man shows him:

Two figures stand on opposite ends of a massive plate, which is balanced on a pinpoint pinnacle. Beneath them: fear, pain, death. The two move about the plate, trying to maintain the balance while simultaneously attempting to upset the other. If one is lost and the other is lucky enough not to be dragged down with him, the only safe place left is in the center, alone, surrounded by emptiness. Or both can come to the center. Or both can simply walk away. Or—

The light goes down on the spine, and the blood runs down the spine. All is black and cold. All is rotten and old. All is a feast for carrion birds. All is lost.

All is lost.

Three separate pieces: flesh and mold, pieced together of their own accord fit imperfectly and tumble down.

Shake.

Tremble.

Shutter.

Groan.

Die.

The Emperor nods. "I see your problem. It is not an easy decision to make."

"But is it possible to co-exist without conflict?"

"Perhaps, but life isn't very interesting without it, either for those involved, or for any who are left by the wayside to observe. Not many thingy-wingies are. In any case, how you feel and how your Nemesis feels are two different matters entirely. For all of his cordiality, he is not as straightforward as he may appear."

"True enough." The man takes another small sip of water. Waits a moment. "So where does that leave us?"

"In need of a climax?" The Emperor shrugs. "I'm not entirely certain. But don't over-analyze everything so much. You are on a journey . . . take each moment as it comes . . . and for now, I say: you need some rest, a bath, a shave— not unless you wish to keep your new beard, of course— and some good food and drink. Your Nemesis can wait a little longer, but know that whatever you decide, I will not intervene for either of you, which is I'm sure what you were wanting to hear."

The man smiles. "Fair enough."

"So that's plenty of chit-chat for now. It's my birthday and I still want to celebrate, even if it's just the two of us. Besides, soon enough, there is going to be one massive funeral to preside over— there were *a lot* of courtiers who didn't make it. But all thingy-wingies in their due time."

The man nods, hesitating for a moment, then: "But one last question, if you don't mind."

"Certainly."

"I don't imagine you have a rune-carved black sword around anywhere?"

The Emperor laughs, holding up his wings.

"I don't even have fingers, much less opposable thumbs. What would I do with a sword? Much less a fancy-wancy antique custom job, hmmm?"

"Just curious."

"Just kidding . . . Actually, I've got him growing dust over the mantle in my private suite. It's a long story about how we first met, and perhaps I'll tell it to you sometime. But for now, suffice it to say that right from the beginning we never got along. And since then he's got my gourd a few too many times, so I keep him there, untouched, stewing and brewing away. And no one else dares to go near the dirty, soul-stealing bugger."

"Him?"

"Oh, that demon is definitely a *him* alright. Just like me, you, the obese tabby. We're all male, and just because the tabby, the sword and I aren't human, there is no reason not to refer to us as *he* and *him*. Humans get so full of themselves sometimes, present company excluded, of course."

"Of course."

"Although, I must admit that the sword is an *it*, too, demon that it is. But then again, he's got too much personality to ignore." The Emperor pauses, a little exasperated. "See what even thinking about that sword does to me."

"I apologize from bringing the matter up."

"Not your fault, how were you to know?" The Emperor smiles knowingly. "I'd smile ironically, but I don't know how . . . Now how about some dinner?"

THE POST-FATALISTIC NOSTALGIA OF VINYL

Aurora. Liquid sunshine streaming down a steel slide across the sky. All is aglow.

The prophet feels each and every drop of perspiration rising to the surface of his skin. Not long before, cool fluid was flowing through his veins, like a blue flame, languid and low, as if it had nowhere to go. But that was in darkness and almost in his death. Fortunately, no life is to be wasted today, thank you very much. Rather, he has survived to face another dawn, beginning with the spectacle above.

He lies in the sand. Burrowed in. Molded. T-shirt rolled under his head, fingers laced over his flat stomach, barely rising and falling. Eyes open. Searching. Divining. Filing the information away, obscure as it is. Then: grinning. Smiling. Laughing. Spitting, but only a little— can't waste it too much. Finally, settling in again.

Resting.

Waiting.

Yes. Another day. Another day filled with unrelenting heat and brilliance and solitude— until he is tempted, of course. But the demons never come at the same time twice. Or maybe they never really leave— simply hanging back, invisible, watching him suffer, rant, pray, starve, hallucinate, build sandcastles, and go insane. In any case, when they do make themselves known to him, they are never big on chit-chat, not unless they're working some angle. However, the results are always the same: the prophet always wants to give in, but something also always sets him off and he sends the demons packing with their tails (tales?) between their legs. Off to torment someone else, no doubt. But the prophet has enough of his own problems without having to worry about someone else's temptations. Besides, so far, the only thing he has found a talent for in the desert is resisting temptations.

Well, that, and building sandcastles; especially when he considers his limited resources, he realizes that he could kick some major butt in a professional beach tournament somewhere.

Anywhere.

But not today.

Today he actually has something else in mind, which is quite a relief for him. There's only so much fasting and praying a prophet can do, and he would live a very happy life if he never had to dream again. *Ever.* But the dreams never end and he certainly can't forget them, even after he records them in his journal. All he hopes for is that the dreams are as significant as they appear to him. Otherwise . . . Otherwise . . . Well there's not much he can do about it either way, but he can only pray that all of his experiences and suffering are serving some purpose. He still can't remember who or what he is a prophet for; so for the time being, he's going to continue doing things his way. At least, as much as he can.

Although, he must admit, he is getting rather tired of building sandcastles. Without any extras, there are only so many ways he can build them before they all start looking the same. For a short time he *did* try making animals, but that made him a little too uneasy. *And hungry.* Sand has no nutritional value, and even less flavor, and it goes down like, well, exactly like sand. Trust him. He knows. Better to stick with the inanimate and inedible, rather than create his own temptations.

Especially not today.

Today he must focus. Concentrate. Sometimes it's impossible, to be sure, with the heat and light radiating all around him, competing with the monotony. But he will do it; otherwise he might as well just lay here and give in. Give up.

Not today.

The prophet stretches in the sand, extending his arms and legs, flexing his fingers and toes, rolling his neck. Soon satisfied, he sits up and runs his fingers through his long, greasy, matted hair, attempting to free it of sand. He brushes off his old, leather flight jacket and picks up his T-shirt, then snaps it a couple times in the breeze. Tying it on his head, he begins to hum and crackle.

His canvas shoulder bag is within his reach, and he takes it up and places it before his crossed legs. Opening it, he inspects its contents: a couple of pens, his journal, a comb, a multi-purpose pocket knife, and a toothbrush. He ate his toothpaste two days ago.

"Now *those* were some hallucinations." Grins.

Scattered throughout are the shattered remains of his misfortune.

And his grin is gone.

If only he hadn't zigged when he should have zagged, he could have avoided his misfortune altogether. But in a way he is glad— he has learned a great deal, and he has met the young woman— without whom he may have been unable to complete his journey to the desert. Still, the pull of his misfortune is incredibly strong sometimes. Only by viewing it as a temptation has he been able to resist it so often in the desert.

Now, however, the prophet willing gives himself over to it, seeking inspiration. Motivation. Increasing the volume in his humming, he reverently takes up several pieces in his hands and holds them up in his open palms. He closes his eyes, but focuses on the image of his misfortune in his hands with his mind. His voice changes pitch as he brings his hands together, working the pieces into one.

The prophet's body trembles and sweat runs down his brow as he feels the power flowing through himself and into his hands. Plastic melts, wires fuse together, and components connect in new ways, all the while taking their toll on his hands, and more. Cut and burned, blood flows from several wounds fuelling the process. Nonetheless, the prophet carries on.

Then, holding the newly formed piece in his left hand, he dips his right into his satchel and draws out another; then later another, and more as his new craft takes shape.

As he continually shapes the new piece, his humming and bleating become more articulate at times.

" . . . thhhirrrrr . . . teeee . . . thhhrrreeee . . . annnnnd . . . ahhh . . . thhhirrrrd . . ."

Only a couple of pieces left. A good thing as the prophet's strength is becoming greatly depleted— his head throbbing, his heart hammering in his chest, fluid flowing freely from his hands, his ears, his eyes.

" . . . forrrrrteeee . . . fiiiivvvvve . . ."

Hands shaking, he takes up the last broken piece from his bag and brings his hands together.

" . . . sevvvvennnnn . . . teeee . . . eighhhht . . ."

Fusing the last one into the new craft in his hands, he cries out:

"I MISS MY TURNTABLE!!!!!!!!!!!!"

And he falls back, unconscious. Almost dead.

Time passes but nothing changes.

Nothing changes.

Until he is awakened some time later, by the watery voice of many.

"Sleeping on the job, prophet? What kind of example are you setting, hmmm?"

The prophet's eyes flutter open and he takes in the constantly shifting features of the demon. Nothing he hasn't seen before, so he takes his time assessing his condition before he decides he actually has the strength to get up from his prone position. Not that he can move that quickly anyway. For, whatever rest he received from being unconscious, he still feels mentally and physically drained from his recent creation. Everywhere, his body aches, as if he had slept in a butter churn or in a garbage compactor that somebody forgot to shut off.

Gradually sitting up, he glances down at his craft on the sand between his legs. He wonders if the demon saw it already, or if it even witnessed its creation earlier. *If so, did the demon try to touch it while he lay unconscious?* After a moment's consideration, the prophet realizes that the demon couldn't touch it even if it wanted to do so.

Grinning, the prophet holds it up towards the demon in his right hand, proudly displaying his craft. Immediately upon touching his craft the prophet feels a little better.

"I've been busy—" The prophet begins, his voice low. Suddenly, he breaks out laughing as he watches the demon recoil in extreme horror from his craft, which looks something like a kaleidoscope, but it is not.

"How did you . . .?"

"Silence! I'm asking the questions, demon."

On a whim, the prophet pockets his craft in his leather jacket, but as he expects, the demon comes no closer. The prophet realizes that it is not simply afraid of his craft, but even more so, it is afraid of *him*.

Without a doubt, he has changed; although in some ways he also feels more like his old self from before he ever arrived in the obese tabby's domain. For that too the prophet feels better, stronger. But still he knows the shadowy, unstable part of his psyche hasn't left him yet either, and he realizes that perhaps it never will. Nonetheless, he finally feels ready to move onward.

The prophet takes up the canvas strap and hooks his satchel over his shoulder and across his chest. Then, slowly, purposefully, he gets up. He stands there woozily for a moment or two, with the demon watching him intensely. It's curious and afraid, but it's also seeking a way back into the prophet. Even though the prophet is physically weak at the moment, the demon knows that he is much more powerful in more important ways than ever. It didn't expect something like this to happen, and unless it can find a way quickly back in, it also knows that it's going to suffer tremendously; making the prophet's suffering look like a day at the beach. But what to do? What to do?

The prophet turns away. "I'm outta here."

The demon's eyes widen in shock. No time. No time. No time. No time. It whirls around in front of the prophet, blocking his path, but without getting too close.

"You can't go. Not yet."

The prophet stops, bemused, but also happy to have a moment to rest. Uncertain how long he can maintain this show of strength, as weak as it is.

"Why not?"

" . . . Ah . . . You haven't even come close to putting in forty days and forty nights. You've barely done half a score. Not even close to the tradition."

The prophet shrugs. "So?"

" . . . *Sooooo* . . . you know why you're here . . . You have an obligation . . . You're not ready yet, not by a long shot . . . Who's going to listen to a prophet that's only done ten days in the desert— that's not very impressive, now is it?"

"That's pride."

"No. That's reality."

"Perhaps, but I don't know that I need to impress anyone anyway. That's not my mission."

" . . . But, ah . . . you don't even know what your mission is, do you? You don't even know whom you're supposed to be prophesying for— how can you leave without knowing that, hmmm?"

The prophet raises an eyebrow. "Do you know the answers to any of those questions?"

"Us? We . . . ah . . ."

"Exactly. So why should I bother wasting any more time with you or your ilk?"

"Why? Because . . . ah . . . ah . . . aren't you giving in to temptation by leaving here before your time is up?"

The prophet considers this: *is he being led astray? Into his temptation: his great desire to leave this place?* A possibility, but still, it feels somehow *right* to go now. There is no temptation, only his *choice* to leave and continue his journey, his mission. Besides:

"If I am doing the wrong thing, why are you trying so hard to stop me?"

The demon stammers. " . . . Ah . . . ah . . . reverse psychology . . . hmmm . . .?"

"Kiss my hairy butt."

The demon drops to its knees, puckering its many lips.

"Yes! Please! Anything! Just don't leave us!"

The prophet remains where he is standing, utterly unmoved by this pathetic display.

"No. That's exactly what I want you to do: *leave me . . . Now.*"

The demon inches its way a little closer to the prophet on its knees. Groveling. Still puckering.

" . . . ah . . . ah . . ."

Furious at being denied, the prophet cries:

"BEGONE!!"

With that, the demon evaporates and drains away, wailing in agony.

Somewhat surprised, but very satisfied, the prophet smiles to himself, until he realizes he doesn't remember which way he came ten very long days and nights ago. He slowly turns around, but there are no differences, no signs. Nothing to guide him. Or so it seems.

"I should have asked for directions before I did that. Not like it would have given me the right ones, anyway. Besides, what good am I if I can't find my way out of here?"

The prophet shrugs, and adjusts the strap of his canvas satchel. With his right hand in his pocket wrapped around his craft, he whistles an old tune and walks into the wind.

SILENT GREEN AND THE NOISE OF CARPET

Morning. Mourning? Yes, for many in The Emperor's Court today, and for numerous days to come. For awhile anyway, until, like almost everyone past, they are eventually forgotten. For The Emperor himself, however, he never began to grieve, so there's nothing to stop. He knows only too well there are countless more where they came from. As always. So time to move onward.

The Emperor waddles slowly through the dense foliage thick with dawn's dew evaporating, as the day grows longer. Warmer. Wearing his shades to keep the brightness of the morn away, he glances up at his companion and makes a sweeping motion with his wing. The man follows the gesture, nodding appreciatively, while adjusting his umbrella to maximize the shade over The Emperor.

"So what do you think?"

The man's gaze falls on the many features: trees, shrubs, vines, flowers, all filled with brilliant colors, with life. So much green. Natural wealth and no envy anywhere. Overlapping and overhanging, but still room for everyone and everything. Acceptance.

He stops— his newly shined shoes sinking in the thick moss— and he savors the comfort, the support. The man sighs, running his fingers under his cleanly shaven chin. Finally, he speaks:

"What can I say?" He smiles sardonically. "I must admit I didn't appreciate it as much when I first arrived. It was a relief to be out of the desert, but the humidity and the foliage became almost as oppressive as I made my way to your palace. In my domain, the weather is more regular: never too hot or too cold, too wet or too dry. And the flora is spread quite thinly. Now, however, I can truly appreciate it all, and I'm very happy to see that you haven't—"

The man hesitates, catching a glimpse of someone in the distance. He sharpens his focus, then filters out every other sound— their breathing, insects buzzing, a soft breeze blowing by, and more. The person is not alone. Standing on the opposite side of a palm tree, he and his companion run a massive saw back and forth across its base. Meanwhile, they are singing rather heartily, accenting each half-line with three quick cuts of the saw:

"Sing a tune and be a bard.
Just do anything, it ain't that hard.
Rob an inn or a shop—
Just don't get caught by a cop.
Kill a man and take his gold
Especially if he's old."

The man frowns, having heard enough, and looks at The Emperor questioningly. The Emperor tries to see what the man is looking at, but his eyesight is too poor even with his prescription sunglasses. He too recognizes that they are singing, but his hearing isn't sharp enough to distinguish the lyrics.

"Why such a face?"

"I was about to say how happy I am to see that you haven't tried to change anything . . ." The man reconsiders his words. "But then again I imagine you need raw materials from time to time. I apologize for judging you. It's not for me—"

"Ahhhh! Tush-tush. They are craftsmen, happy in their work, which you see and hear. They are almost always singing some lusty loony tune . . ." The Emperor pauses, noting the man's odd expression hasn't changed. "Truly, I try to leave as much unspoiled as possible, but after such a massive funeral as yesterday's, we need to re-stock as quickly as possible. But don't worry, we recycle everything. Why do you think I wanted to take you on this walk today?"

The man's frown deepens. He searches around, seeing many other craftsmen working in the far distance: cutting down trees, gathering leaves, flowers, berries, moss, and more. All are smiling. Many are singing. None are silent.

The Emperor pats him on the arm. "Why, to ease your conscience, of course. To show you that even after such a loss, nothing is wasted."

"Please pardon my lack of understanding, but—"

The Emperor chuckles. "Where do you think my Court comes from?"

"Indeed?" The man finally raises his eyebrows. Cracks a slight grin. "I've seen the strings, but I never would have believed that your courtiers were actually constructed of—"

"Explains a lot, doesn't it? Ehwhatnot. But truth be told, they're actually quite different just after they're made— not much unlike the vibrant life you see around you— colorful, innocent, filled with wonder, and their own individual delights. But somewhere along the way, in their education, their upbringing, they become as you have seen many of them: proud, greedy, twisted, cynical, and even incredibly stupid. Many appear to be working towards the well being of the many, but ultimately they are only self-serving. And perhaps the worst part is, it seems it gets worse with each new generation. Of course, part of the problem may be that we *are* recycling— shredding, composting, and sending them back to the soil after they die. Perhaps it's going wrong right from the ground up— some unaccounted for ehwhatnot . . . I suppose that's what we get for being all hoighty-toighty pish-posh, trying to create in our own images. It's so easy now to create life, manipulate it in whatever way we please, but to nurture it, love it, give it the attention it needs . . ."

The Emperor turns away with his head down.

"But you didn't start all of this, did you?"

"No. But I didn't stop it either. I've perpetuated it to fulfil my own selfish and greedy needs, as well as the expectations of those around me." The Emperor glances back at the man. "Well, so much for trying to ease *your* conscience . . ."

The man shakes his head. "Have no fears for my well-being. I have experienced much worse things . . . been a part of—"

"Tush-tush. Let's hear no more on it. If you are past it, then I'll not push the matter any further."

"Very well. Shall we return then, or do you wish to continue?"

"Would you care to see the workshops?" The Emperor points away into the distance, where the man sees a cluster of cottages with a stream running nearby. A great number of people are scurrying about, their arms full.

"I thought you weren't—"

"Just kidding . . . You're always so serious, but never mind. Let's return. At my pace, we'll be lucky to make it back for lunch, but we'll have quite the appetite, I'm sure . . . I knew we should have brought a snack— at least a few crullers and some port. Ah, well."

The Emperor waddles past the man and begins to cross back towards his palace in the opposite direction of the workshops. Stepping up beside him, the man continues to shelter The Emperor with his umbrella. Meanwhile, his newly pressed suit is soaking through from his sweat and from the heavy dew rubbing off on him. But the man has no complaints.

They walk for some time in warm silence until they come upon a fern almost as tall as the man. The Emperor stops and affectionately brushes at the leaves. He stays there for some time, inspecting it, counting the branches, flicking away insects. The man stands beside him, saying nothing.

"See what has grown from the remains of my first chancellor . . . It's, *he's* not all bad is he?"

The man puts a comforting arm around The Emperor, who leans against him and quivers.

"We have far less control over others than we think, *especially* over those who are close to us. Why do we get caught up in such futile games?"

The man decides to stay silent.

The Emperor snorts derisively and drops his wings to his sides.

Mutters: "Games?"

The man also takes his arm away and faces The Emperor.

"Who is pulling the strings?"

The Emperor regards him for a moment, then grins, his mirth slowly returning.

"I don't know."

"Truly?"

"As you know only too well, things are different here. I may have become The Emperor with my own skills and a dash of good fortune, ehwhatnot, but this palace was already here, and much of my Court was already established with many others nearby . . . Waiting for me or for someone else, I don't know."

"You don't feel manipulated at all? Then, or now?"

The Emperor holds out his wings. "See: no strings attached. Besides, no one forced me to become The Emperor. Having many things already established before I arrived was a little unsettling, but I've never really bothered to ask. Nor do I really care. Someone else — or perhaps some*thing* else, I suppose — is pulling the strings in my Court, true enough, but all is well . . . All is . . ."

"But whatever happened to the previous ruler?"

The Emperor shrugs. "Retired? In hiding, pulling the strings? Deceased? Assassinated? Believe me, I've thought of these thingy-wingies, and I've asked around, of course, but no one knows, or at least no one is talking. Still, I have no real fears for myself. I'm a fair, just, and lusty ruler. I've led a good life. My subjects are content. When my time comes, in whatever form, I will go with no misgivings."

The man nods and remains silent. Contemplative. The Emperor eyes him for a minute, then breaks the silence once again.

"Why all the questions? Are you afraid of someone or something pulling your strings? Manipulating you and everyone around you for their own purposes?"

"Never before, but perhaps now . . ."

"Pish-posh! You're your own man. You do what you choose."

"No more. No less."

"Exactly. But again, you're thinking too much. Always considering all the angles, ehwhatnot? If you wish to confront the obese tabby, then confront him. *Now*. If not, then stay. *Relax*. Continue to enjoy my hospitality. Or return to your own realm if you so desire. Whatever the consequences are, they will occur in their own time. But enough thinking— you should act now."

"Then perhaps I should be on my way."

The Emperor's stomach rumbles. "But after lunch, of course. Can't send a man out on an empty stomach."

The man smiles his consent. "Of course." Raises his umbrella over The Emperor. "Shall we?"

The Emperor nods and begins to waddle back towards his castle. Their trail broken somewhat, their return is easier, and The Emperor actually picks up his pace as his hunger grows. After a short while, his stomach growls and gurgles almost constantly.

The man does his best to hold in his laughter, even though his own stomach is just as empty. Going hungry is rarely an issue for him, but he enjoys The Emperor's company and has no wish to offend him. Another excellent meal is more than welcome, particularly since he has decided to confront the obese tabby. The man speculates about when he will eat again after lunch, if ever. And thinking about lunch reminds him of his stop at Ego Sideroad's in the obese tabby's memory. He wonders about how the young woman is doing and if he will see her again, as well.

The man shakes his head, suppressing a laugh. The Emperor is right: he is *always* thinking, considering every ehwhatnot. But he can't help it. Nor does he believe he would change that aspect of himself, even though he could. No. Before he considers anything else, however, The Emperor breaks into his thoughts.

"If you don't mind me asking, have you cracked the seal on The Prize yet?"

"No. Not yet."

"Will you do it before you leave?"

"What would you like to know?"

"I am curious . . . and perhaps . . ."

"Perhaps, I'll pass something on to you?"

"Perhaps . . . No matter, I suppose. But why have you hesitated for so long?"

The man stops and considers his question for a moment while The Emperor looks up at him expectantly.

Until finally: "A long time ago, an underling asked me: 'If I could have

complete knowledge of anything at all— what would I want to know about?'
I thought about it for a moment and I answered: 'Complete knowledge
about whether or not there was any kind of existence after we die, and if
there is, what exactly is that existence?'"

The Emperor nods. "A good answer. But I still don't understand—"

"I'm uncertain if that's the kind of knowledge, the kind of power I want
to possess. How would it change me? How would I treat others? How would
I look back upon my past? Sometimes too much knowledge can be a dangerous thing. With that kind of knowledge—"

The Emperor holds up his wings, stopping him.

"Say no more on it. I understand." He waddles onward, wanting to break
the uneasy moment and trying to hide the last thunderous rumble in his
belly. "Just out of curiosity, did you ask him the same question in return?"

"Yes." The man falls into step beside him. "I wasn't certain at first if he
was joking or not when he asked me the question, or if there was a particular
answer he had in mind. And in any case, I was curious."

"And what was his response? What did he want to have complete knowledge about?"

"Women . . . women . . ."

The Emperor nods knowingly and the two continue on their way to the
palace, each burrowing deeply into his own thoughts.

MILEAGE ON THE KNEES

Midday. Lunch. Bell ringing in the distance. Hammer rapping repeatedly. Warning? For the wave? The surge? The shouts? But they don't come. Not today. No. Looking back. Not for quite some time.

No matter. The prophet would still rather be alone for the moment, anyway. On his belly, he lays on the dune observing the rear of the building, still uncertain whether or not it is another mirage before him. Or worse: another test.

The demons didn't give in as easily as he first believed. All along his journey across the desert, they returned to him, albeit at a respectable distance, but always with a new offer, a new temptation. But he refused them. Even as he grew physically weaker, he became stronger spiritually, feeding off their looks of defeat, enjoying hearing the failure in the watery voices of many. Although, each time, they became more desperate, their promises grander, and each time he considered giving in a little more. But in the end, he still refused, knowing that they wouldn't be so desperate unless he was getting closer to his destination, both physically and spiritually.

But here, now, looking at the back of the yellow bricked two story building, he wonders if he went the right way after all. He doesn't really remember the building, at least in his recent travels. Perhaps from long ago, but certainly not in this desert, and especially not with all of the graffiti. *Had the demons left him alone only recently, so that he might stumble upon their lair unwittingly?*

The bell stops, but the ringing persists as a shadow in his memory. *An awakening?* He can't say. *An annoyance?* Somewhat. But no worse than the watery voices of many swishing and buzzing in his ears.

The prophet jots a few notes in his journal regarding this last leg of his journey, then puts it away. He can write more later *after* he's off the sand and away from the intense heat. His new visions are scorched in his mind and they aren't about to leave him unscarred any time soon. Just like all the others. Lucky for him.

He draws himself up, scanning the barred but broken windows, searching for any signs of life: lights, voices, movement, anything, but there is nothing. Eventually he stands on unsteady legs, and removes the T-shirt from his head and wipes his face and neck. After loosely folding the T-shirt and putting it in his canvas shoulder bag, the prophet finally takes a step towards the building.

Sand sifts into the gravel and the small islands of ancient asphalt, which make up the parking lot. A high chain link fence lines the perimeter, topped with razor wire, and the prophet is faced with the task of climbing it. He exhales a small sigh of despair, knowing he can't do it, especially with the razor wire present. But as the last of that breath is released, he realizes that the demons heard his sigh and they will return all too soon.

So, determined, he darts his eyes around searching for any opening. Fortunately, he soon spots one around the corner. This he can do and, in this small triumph, he feels the demons slipping away just as quickly, knowing that he won't bow to them now.

Supporting himself against the fence, he drags his steps, rounds the corner, and raises the latch on the gate. Enters the lot. Why the gate isn't locked, the prophet doesn't know or care. He's simply happy that, with each step he takes, the desert will be that much farther behind him.

There are no vehicles of any type to be seen, only junk food wrappers, crushed pop containers, and cigarette butts are scattered across the lot. As well, here and there exist small craters surrounded by a scattering of old wind worn bones, mostly human. The prophet tries to make a note of this, but nothing sinks in too deeply in his heat soaked brain.

Stepping closer to the building, he pauses, reading some of the messages scrawled, including:

THIS NEW SCHEDULE SUCKS!!

And:

WHERE ARE YOUR PRINCIPALS????

And:

JUST ADD FANTASY— MAKES ITS OWN REALITY!!

And even two haiku:
EUTHANASIA

MAN AT HIS KEYBOARD
TYPING OVER AND OVER
THUNDERSTORM LIGHTNING

And:

HAIKU WANNABE
HAIKU WANNABE — YOU SUCK
TO THE NTH DEGREE

After several minutes of attempting to divine the overlapping phrases and artwork, the prophet is still uncertain whether or not he's to take some special meaning from anything. The haiku seems almost familiar and he is struck with a sense of deja vu: standing here like this once before, but also that he was here when the haiku was first written; that perhaps he was the writer of both. But the moment slips away, the shadow of the memory forgotten, and he only stands there dazed and confused.

A soft breeze slips by, picking up some of the papers along with it. The prophet lazily follows them with his eyes and begins to step forward. Suddenly, he notices several gray metal "buttons" buried. He hesitates, searching the lot, finding more and more. It takes him a minute, but then he realizes that the parking lot is mined. Although he can see bits of many of them, he knows that there are likely a great deal more he can't see.

Holding his place, he twists his head around. Yes, he is surrounded, and it is perhaps only a miracle that has brought him this far into the lot. He sees where there were a number of close calls— once, way too close— even in the short distance he has traveled so far across the lot.

The prophet considers his few options, knowing he can't stay where he is and hope to be rescued. And while it might be easier to return the way he came, there is no guarantee he would make it. Besides, he has absolutely no desire to return to the desert.

So, senses reaching, praying for deliverance— even though he still doesn't remember who he is supposed to be praying to— the prophet cautiously navigates his way through the minefield. He approaches the small shadowed alcove set into the rear of the building, hoping the doors at the bottom of the short flight of stairs will be unlocked. If not, he would rather try to climb the building than go back through the parking lot. Too soon, however, he becomes afraid to look where he is stepping. Instead he focuses on the almost hidden doors, relying on his faith to carry him across.

Then, with the stairs almost within reach, the double doors at the bottom of the stairs burst open. The prophet freezes, terrified, and he almost shrinks a size as he sees a small gang of Goons pour out the doors. Immediately, they sense his presence and they too freeze momentarily.

The prophet holds his ground, wondering if this is the trap he's been expecting. What to do? What to do? Goons before him. Mines surrounding him. Nothing but desert beyond, even if he were to escape the first two. So nothing left to do, but:

"Hey!"

The five Goons carefully ascend the stairs, then spread out on the small extension of concrete. Silently, they communicate back and forth. So far, thankfully, no weapons appear, and the prophet simply stands his ground. Wisely, he says nothing more. Then, after a minute, the Goons part ways, apparently for the prophet to pass by. However, there is still some ground between them, and the prophet realizes that they may be simply waiting to see if he makes it the rest of the way. If he doesn't, well, no problem— they may just need to clean themselves off a bit. If he does, he will have nowhere to run and he will be at their mercy; which even in his short experience with Goons, he knows doesn't exist.

Trembling, but eyes forward, the prophet crosses the rest of the way over the lot and onto the concrete, unscathed. Suppressing a sigh, he waits for the Goons to make their move. As expected, they come together around him and appear to grow taller and wider, intimidating him. Planting their feet. Leather creaking. Weapons— short pipes, makeshift knives, and links of rusty chains— slide into their gloved hands.

Resolved to pass by, the prophet finally releases his sigh, then steps forward, frowning. Slowly shaking his head, he walks purposefully towards them while they close their circle. Until he utters:

"I just knew this was going to happen."

Immediately, the Goons stop closing in and, when the prophet reaches the Goon directly in front of him, the Goon steps aside at the last moment and allows him to pass, untouched. Eyes straight ahead, the prophet descends the stairs, relishing each step into the increasingly cool darkness. Behind him, he hears the weapons being replaced, and the strange, quiet, inarticulate sounds, which the prophet is certain is their form of laughter. They can laugh all they want as far as he is concerned. He admits his fear, and he is more than glad that he is alive to do so.

Reaching the bottom of the stairs, the prophet wastes no time, but pulls both doors open and enters the relatively cool, unlit hallway. Shivering for a moment, he walks slowly while his eyes adjust. The doors click shut behind him, closing him off from the Goons. He only hopes their mood doesn't change and they come after him.

The prophet draws up his right hand and searches for the wall beside him. Finding the cold, painted bricks with his worn, dry fingers, he trails them along to help keep his bearings. As he walks cautiously down the long hallway, he occasionally sniffs the air, expecting the redolence of refuse and decay, but he smells very little. Thus far, the hallway is quite dusty and there is some garbage, but there is far less than in the prophet's travels in the obese tabby's domain. So, he hopes he is still on the right track.

Just ahead, he hears garbled voices and he soon comes upon a junction. With his eyes becoming accustomed to the darkness, he sees the main hallway continues forward. To either side, there is a short corridor with a dim outline of double doors at each end. Stopping and listening, he finds the voices are coming from the left. The prophet goes down the short hallway, his fingers hissing against the cinder blocks until he reaches the double doors. The voices grow louder, but they are no more distinctive than before.

Like the double doors he originally came through, these also have small windows. So, rather than entering, the prophet peers through a window, hoping to catch some glimpse, even though it appears to be almost as dark on the other side of the glass.

Suddenly, the lights snap on and he draws his hands up to cover his eyes. Blinking rapidly, trying to clear his vision once again, he listens intently, expecting the Goons to round the corner and grab him. Then, keeping his hands over his eyes, he opens the lids and slowly parts his fingers, allowing the light to filter in.

As images form around him, there is a hearty burst of laughter and the prophet stumbles backward, wondering where the Goons finally found their vocal cords. The prophet drops his hands and regains his balance while he darts his eyes around. He's no longer before the doors, but rather, he's in the room he was peering into only moments before. The doors are at the top of a flight of stairs across the Industrial Arts shop. The smell of cut wood and burnt metal is in the air. Half-finished cedar chests and maple rocking chairs are spread over the worktables, but all the saws, sanders, and other machines are off.

Now, he is standing around the perimeter of a small circle with another gang of Goons. No. Wait. Not Goons. Much smaller. Teenagers. Dressed similarly in denim and T-shirts, runners, and a couple whose parents can afford leather jackets for them. Rough, but relatively clean. Raunchy, but nowhere nearly as tough as they would like to believe.

No one seems to take any notice of his sudden appearance. Nor do they question him stepping in amongst them again, even though he's twice their age and he looks like he's just spent forty days and nights in the desert. Well, more or less. Actually, it was only ten, but who's counting? He wonders about how they see him, or if they see him at all.

Again, there is a burst of laughter and the prophet finds himself laughing along with them; although, he can't understand why. He looks to the center of the circle, where a bespectacled, balding, fat old man stands, with his brown, polyester pants hitched high over his rather large belly. The teacher holds an oxy-acetylene torch in one cigarette-stained hand and a striker in the other. Another student asks another stupid question, which is met with an even louder bout of laughter as the teacher fumbles through his response; uncertain if they are laughing at him or not, and knowing there is something he is forgetting.

In mid-laugh the prophet sees what the teacher is missing: he turned on the gases a short time ago and they are filling the room. Each time the teacher moves to ignite the torch, someone else asks another question, as the gases flow.

And flow.

Finally, it seems no one has any more silly questions or comments, and the teacher makes his move, still unmindful of the gases. His sides hurting from all the laughter, his lungs full of oxygen and acetylene, the prophet leaps forward to stop him; only to find himself holding the torch and snapping the striker as he watches a wide-eyed student leaping at him. There is a brilliant flash. Everyone's eyebrows disappear, and then their faces, and then—

The prophet is standing in another room: same concrete floor, same butter-colored brick walls, but these are covered with poorly painted abstracts, collages of torn magazine pages, and pasted geometric shapes of construction paper. Coat hanger mobiles and papier mache masks hang from the ceiling. He no longer holds the torch and striker, but rather, a small pair of blunt-nosed scissors and a paintbrush covered with mind-numbing glue. The prophet almost stabs himself with both items as he feels his face, happy to know he hasn't been burned to a crisp.

Calming himself, he takes in the two new teens standing before him. A girl: fake-baked and flat chested, with only her ego to inflate it along with her many other delusions of pubescent grandeur. A boy: gap-toothed, freckled runt, but "oh so cool." Punk. Both come from wealthy families, of course. They lean together over her collage, snickering, too good to be wasting their time with such an exercise, but not having the nerve to cut class. Neither takes any notice of the prophet.

She whines. Speaks through her pug nose. "I just don't know what to do with this . . . Something isn't quite right."

The curly-haired runt leans in some more. Nudges her. Whispers almost conspiratorially:

"Why don't you bleed on it?"

The two giggle and bump against one another. The prophet joins in with their snickering, perhaps a little too loudly. They take notice of him, scowling the whole time, and again, the prophet wonders about what they are seeing. They don't appear to find him out of the ordinary. Unwanted, yes, but not totally unexpected.

Forgetting himself, he misinterprets the supposed source of the blood and manages, his voice crackling:

"That's sick. I mean that's really sick. That's really sick, man."

Their scowls deepen; the punk's de-evolving into a sneer.

He barks: "Aw, shut up! Who asked you, anyway?"

The prophet goes cold. His moment of perverse mirth forgotten. His fingers tighten around the scissors and the paintbrush. Caught up in the moment, he does his own leaning. Rage growing, solidifying. Suddenly snapping, but his voice is low. Arctic.

"Well, no one, I guess. But now how would you like to bleed for me?"

The prophet leaps forward, his arms outstretched, art supplies in hand.

And he finds himself bumping into another kid altogether, who bumps into the person ahead of him, who bumps into another and so forth. Some of the teens grunt and groan, but soon the domino wave is over and it's quickly forgotten.

Everyone, including him, holds a bottom-of-the-line acoustic guitar. Everyone, vaguely familiar, though the prophet remembers no one's name. Everyone— thirty students or more— is in a row waiting to have them tuned. Only one teacher performs this function and there is a perpetual twanging of out-of-tune strings: ping-ping-ping . . . pong-pong-pong . . . Over and over and over. As each student gets in tune then takes his or her seat, the guitar in question is almost out-of-tune again from the simple transportation, and from the occasional tentative strumming and plucking of the strings along the way.

. . . ping-ping-ping . . .

. . . pong-pong-pong . . .

Again and again and again and—

The line moves . . . infrequently, and the prophet glances down at his own borrowed guitar. He takes it up uncertainly, knowing he should be able to tune it himself and play it with ease. But suddenly, he has no memory of how to do a simple open A or G or a basic barre chord. So instead, he strums the open strings with his index finger and meets with an unsettling jangle of notes. Another memory jars and he realizes that he doesn't know how to play *yet* in this room, that he learns *later*. Although, again from his perspective— that he is still himself— he should be able to play now anyway, but he can't remember what to do.

Frustrated, he leans the guitar against the wall. Despite his agitation, he doesn't even consider smashing it. Cheap and out-of-tune it may be, but he would rather kill someone than destroy a guitar. Rather, the prophet heads for the open doorway, with another bright hallway leading away from him.

As he passes through the doorway, he finds himself in a classroom with thin, traffic weary, slate gray carpet under his feet. More than a score of students are seated before him. All are blank-faced and appear to be waiting for him to do something. A few focus their bored and resentful eyes upon him, while most are looking anywhere except at him. He wonders what is expected of him when he feels a small stack of papers in his hands.

The prophet looks down at them. Apparently he is supposed to read a story he wrote: "SCORE ME A BENNY." Grade A material according to the teacher. He flips through the pages, trying to remember anything at all, but comes up empty.

He glances around the room again. Nothing changes. Nothing changes. Then he looks at the teacher: a plain, but somehow severe older woman, who is fixing him with a rather petulant glare. She nods at the papers, wanting him to begin. The prophet nods back at her, then turns on his heels and heads for the door. He holds onto the story, hoping he'll get to keep it, so he can read it for himself later. Figure things out. Remember. Something.

But he is denied, of course, and instead, he finds himself standing in the boys' locker room, holding a coarse, urine-colored towel. All around him are pimple-faced naked and semi-naked boys, each with a similar towel. The prophet remains in his same clothes. Still filthy. Dusty. Worn out.

In the center of the room, the Phys Ed instructor is speaking sharply:

"Now you boys have worked up a good sweat today, and there's plenty more days where that came from, let me tell you . . . Now I know all about the horror stories you boys hear about what goes on in the showers, and let me tell you that I won't hear of it this year. Forget about it! There's nothing to worry about. Not while I'm around here . . . So, I'll be checking up on you boys, and let me tell you . . . *Everyone* and I mean *EVERYONE* showers. I don't care who you think you are or where you got to be afterwards, or what you think you have or don't have . . . *Everyone showers!* Now I'll be checking those towels and every single one of them better be wet . . . Alright! Now time's wasting boys! Shower up!"

Despite the strange speech, the idea of a shower has an overwhelming appeal to the prophet. However, he takes no chances and, towel in hand, he keeps his clothes on for the moment. He wants to be certain he'll actually be able to stay in the shower room before he'll strip down.

Ahead of him he hears the relieving musical flow of the water rushing. The prophet lets out a pleasurable sigh and breathes in the moist air. He halts, almost gagging as he really smells himself for the first time in a long time. No one else notices either his odd appearance or his heavy odor, so he keeps crossing over to the showers. Steam rises and he enters the shower room, taking off his canvas satchel.

But once again, the prophet is denied. Steam is still rising, but it's from the massive stockpots across the room. The air is thick with burning canola oil and countless voices. He finds himself with a tray in one hand, standing in another line. Resigned, he replaces his shoulder bag, then takes up his tray in both hands. Like many of those around him, he is waiting for his fries and fish sticks— *sticks* being the operative word. The prophet glances down at his tray, inspecting the soggy scoop of coleslaw oozing across his small Styrofoam saucer. He remembers he always *used to* like coleslaw, even the stuff they ground up for fast food restaurants, but now—

Fish and chips in hand— *chips of what?* The prophet wonders as he waddles and bumps his way through the line in order to pay. As he turns to face the cashier he finds all of the students gone along with his lunch. Or rather, most of the students have gone while all the others are grown. Aged. Those remaining appear to be roughly the same age as the prophet. Their overall wardrobe hasn't really changed at all, and neither are they much different. Everyone has more lines in their faces, less hair on their heads, more fat on their bodies and very few seem to be any happier.

Before the prophet, a table stands a few steps away. Spread out on it are stacks of nametags and a raffle bin with rolls of blood red and bone ivory tickets. Seated behind the table are two pretty, but rather plain women— both dressed casually in jeans and simple blouses— whom he recognizes from the music class. They both smile politely at him, recognition in their eyes as well.

The slim brunette on the left opens up, holding up a nametag.

"Why *hello*! How have you been? It's been *some time*, hasn't it?"

He simply nods and pins on the nametag without even glancing at it, not caring if it's the right one or not. Managing a weak smile of his own, the prophet wonders when this will all end. *When and where will he finally find an exit?* The prophet doesn't even want to consider the possibility he won't find one eventually. He leaves the women at the table, not wanting to be drawn into any idle chit-chat, and shifts his gaze around the cafeteria.

"Don't you want to get some raffle or drink tickets?" The other woman asks.

Again, the prophet doesn't reply, and he simply walks away.

However many years may have passed, everyone has been able to re-establish their cliques very quickly. Cheesy, decadent pop music crackles thinly in the background while more polite, uninteresting conversations ensue. The prophet is able to pick up bit and pieces here and there as he begins to make his rounds: seeking some answers and a way out if he can.

From once circle:

"Me? Same job I had when I was here. Same position. Same car. Still living at home, too, in the basement. No wife. No girlfriend. Not interested . . . That about sums it up, I guess . . . Did you see last night's game?"

To another:

"Me? You know that coleslaw they used to have here and at all those fast food chicken places . . . well, I work in this small town where they make that stuff by the five-gallon pail and ship it out. I've been doing it for a couple of years now, but I'm getting out of it pretty quick though . . . I've got another job lined up, involving septic tanks . . . but I really don't want to talk about that right now . . . And *no*, no husband or boyfriend— no time for a man really."

And another:

"Me? Basically, I take care of a massive freezer. Yeah. That's it. That's my life. Well, I'm married, too, but that's my life: keeping that freezer running five days a week, with three weeks off each year to look forward to until I finally retire in another thirty-seven years."

And the prophet has heard enough. There's plenty more to hear and to see, with new people arriving a few at a time, and no one seems to be going anywhere. But he has had his fill. Definitely. He wants a way out to the time he knows, even if he means he has to go back into the desert, and he wants it *now*.

He crosses the room, heading for a door marked *EXIT*, while somebody calls out behind him trying to flag him down. Ignoring the pleas, thinking it to be the watery voice of many, the prophet increases his pace until he is almost running and he bursts through the door. Outside.

The prophet is outside, under a black cloud-covered sky. People are everywhere. Running and calling. Buying and selling. Wheeling and dealing. But no one is focused on him, and he's glad to be back at The Carnival. Lights flash. Rides roar. Voices and music fill the air. All is as he remembers it to be.

He glances back, wondering what he will see this time, or if he'll simply find himself in another classroom again. Before him, elaborately painted in broad gaudy colors, a mural stands with a single door set into the wall. Depicted is a plethora of undead: vampires, mummies, ghouls, ghosts: all tormenting youthful, solid-jawed heroes and cleavage bursting heroines. Scared, scarred and bleeding, but they still have some hope in their eyes. Boldly painted across the whole mosaic is the legend:

"WELCOME TO THE HOUSE OF HORRORS!"

The prophet is not surprised at all. He is simply overjoyed to be finally free of the place. Nor is he surprised to see a demon, faces blurring, standing before the open door to the Horror House, snickering at him.

"You still have *a lot* to learn, *prophet*. Hopefully, for your sake, you learned something today, but we're betting against it, of course."

The prophet holds his ground. "Of course . . . and *who* exactly is betting on me then?"

The snickering stops, but the demon lets the question go unanswered. Uneasy. Angry. It raises its hackles a little and clears its throats:

"Just so you know, we're not letting you go so easily yet. In fact, we'll probably never let you go. A real challenge is always welcome— makes it all the more worthwhile in the end."

The demon smiles sharply. Toothily. Triumphant evil in its many eyes. Hackles bristling. But the prophet simply shrugs.

"Sometimes a man needs his demons— keeps him on his toes. Helps keep perspective . . . You'll lose your bet, demon . . . I'll figure things out eventually. Now *begone*."

With that, the prophet turns away, while the demon's smile painfully evaporates along with the rest of its body. Maintaining an air of confidence— which he doesn't entirely feel— the prophet has someone he needs to meet, and he hopes he isn't too late.

GRIND TO THE SLAVE

Dawn. Swirls like chilled grenadine and freshly squeezed orange juice float in the air. 100% pulp included, of course. Stirred by a strong breeze, the swirls soon dance and reform new partnerships repeatedly. What metamorphoses a new day brings. But eventually they dissipate; although their sweetness is never lost entirely.

The man stands on a stony summit— observing all of this and more: the mountain range stretching out in all directions. He is not alone. Not exactly. All around him, many of the other great masses are heaped with life and death.

One mountain is simply composed of people, primates, and everyone else in between the evolutionary scale: living, dead, and otherwise. Piled a mile high. Everyone shouting and spitting at each other, but few seem to be speaking the same language. There doesn't even appear to be any attempt at understanding. Calling and crawling. Clawing and climbing. Buying and bribing. Cunning. Lots of cunning. And blood. Always lots of blood, of course, flowing downward in dense streams— its metallic redolence heavy in the air. No concern whatsoever for who is stepped on and trampled underfoot. All attempt to reach the top, only to be inevitably tossed and tumbled to their deaths.

The man focuses on the peak for a minute, initially unsure if his eyes are deceiving him or not. He can't see anything at all special about being on top, but still that's where everyone has their sights set.

The man is glad he works alone.

Observing the mass, the man whispers softly while a brisk wind rushes past him and carries his words away towards it. A minute later, in the distance, there is hesitation, a brief moment of silence, but soon, too soon, the people and the primates continue with their quest for the top.

He has seen enough.

Time to go.

But first, the man briefly consults his works, making calculations, nodding his head in understanding. Relatively satisfied, he gently caresses it with his right thumb before pocketing it again.

Definitely enough.

Definitely time to go.

The man turns to the rough trail behind him, but he is stopped by a hollow voice coming up the mountain from behind some massive boulders.

"Enjoying the view?"

Then.

Presence.

Emerging carefully from behind the rocks, the figure tips his rumpled Stetson and briefly flashes his hourglass grin. He steps forward and the two face off; with the figure's one hand resting lightly upon his crowbar, while his other fingers dance across the smooth steel grip of his nail puller. Cautiously, the man places his small suitcase with his umbrella between the handles on the stony summit. He tilts his head towards the *homo* mound, but never takes his eyes off of the figure.

"See for yourself."

The figure glances past the man, equally unimpressed and unhappy about the landscape around them. Nonetheless, he can't help but snicker.

"Those guys trying to bribe with the bananas just crack me up."

The man nods his ascent, but holds his ground.

"So we are finally met."

"Indeed. And well met." The figure's eyes lock on the man's own. "But Showdown? You bet."

"So soon?"

"Soon?" The figure snorts. "Do you have any idea how long I've been waiting for you in the obese tabby's domain?"

The man barely shrugs.

"For quite some time, let me tell you, and frankly, I got tired of waiting for you to return. I don't know what's come over me lately, but I've never before spent so much time waiting . . . and these sweeping feelings of nostalgia . . . and all these colloquialisms . . . I just—"

"Things are different here."

The figure takes a deep breath and calms himself again. But still, his fingers almost blur at times on the handle of his nail puller.

"Truly. So they are . . . In any case, I wanted to confront you before you . . . *everything* . . . got too far out of hand. Although from what I understand you've been very busy with your time already."

"Oh you know, I've just been here and there, in between."

"Indeed? Care to elaborate?"

"I imagine we should take care of our business here first."

"And then we shall see?"

"Exactly."

The two step closer together, still eyeing one another. Each waits for the other to make the first move. Closer. The figure's fingers dance while the man's arms stay at his sides. Closer. Within striking distance. Closer. On the edge of each other's space. Closer. The man reaches out with his right hand and—

The figure holds out his own and they shake warmly. Then, reaching around with their other arms, they hug firmly, patting each other on their backs. Drawing away, the two lock their hands on the other's forearms and eye each other up and down— noting their many similarities, and a few differences, of course. The figure is taller, leaner, and is perhaps fifteen to twenty years older than the man. But neither says anything in particular to call attention to the fact that they are in many ways basically the same man.

"You look good." The man grins.

"You look better."

"Thank you. But I'm not as well-traveled as you, of course."

"True enough." The two part, but remain where they are standing. "But now we travel together. For a short while at least . . . You have unfinished business with the obese tabby?"

"Yes . . . Yes . . ."

"And The Prize?"

" . . . Still sealed."

The figure raises an eyebrow. "Indeed? Care to explain?"

"I'm still uncertain . . . Do I really want to have the knowledge, the power that The Prize possesses?"

"Why wouldn't you? You knew what was at stake before you entered your works in The Fray, correct?"

The man nods.

"Why else enter it, unless you wanted to win?" The figure tilts his head, scrutinizing. "Unless you simply wanted to keep The Prize from the obese tabby . . . A possibility?"

Nods again.

"So what now? Were you simply planning on giving it away and facing the obese tabby on more even terms?"

Grins. "I almost did give it away."

The figure's eyes widen. "Really? To whom?"

"A prophet in the desert, who bore a striking resemblance to me— well, to us— which neither of us could explain; although neither of us really tried that hard. In any case, he would've seen my offer as a temptation at that time, so I didn't bother. Besides, I believe he may already possess some of the knowledge and the power of The Prize."

"Indeed? Well, it looks like it was a good idea for me to intercept you rather than wait any longer. Who knows what you could do next?"

"Or what I've already done." Raises an eyebrow.

"Indeed." The figure steps back and takes out his art, which he centers on his right index finger.

Balances.

All is.

"We should be on our way. You have much to explain and I have a lot of work to do."

"With me?"

Pockets his art. Nods. "Maintenance."

"Do you have idea how much I hate PR and all that it entails?"

"I feel the same way, but—"

"I know. You're a carpenter. It's what you do."

"Well, so far I haven't been able to do too much of anything— not to my satisfaction, certainly not like usual. There's something about these domains . . . but we shall see how everything comes together. There's much left to consider . . . much to keep in mind for the future—"

"For posterity?"

The figure cracks his hourglass grin while the man crosses over to his things. Takes up his small suitcase. Uses his umbrella like a casual cane. But then, hesitation.

"You know that I usually work alone . . . So, what if I was to refuse? Have I no choice in the matter? Or, what if I were simply to return to my own realm, leaving things as they are?"

The figure regards him, quiet sadness creasing his weathered face even more.

Softly: "There are always choices, of course, even when it doesn't seem apparent. But in your case . . . there's so much more at stake, and even though you could refuse, I believe more harm than good would come from such a decision. So, I highly recommend you take my advice . . . Besides, I was only half-joking about a showdown earlier, but—"

"Say no more. I understand . . . Just curious." Crossing over. "Shall we be on our way then?"

The figure gestures and the man passes by. Then the figure falls into step beside the man as they make their way down the trail.

Ahead of them, a short distance away, another mountain is composed of collectible compost: cards, cups, caps, cyclopedias, stamp books, stuffed animals, dolls and action figures. All of these things and more. Endless amounts of information, memories, media; however selectively true they may be. All moldy, smoldering. The whole mountain is drawn into itself: pulsing with a life of its own. All of the middlemen cut out long ago. Forgotten. Rather, the memorabilia searches out their kindred, trading amongst themselves. Forming and reforming, with no cash involved. Seeking an ultimate *gestalt* together.

Here, the two see they have no place, but neither wants it and they simply move on down the trail. Both are glad that they travel light and that they never got into collecting anything in the first place. No need to be tempted now.

Later in the morning, coming around a bend, they see a third mountain, which is a mass of dissonant sound bites and blinking lights, live wires but dead channels. Topped with countless spires and totems composed of their black and white metal and plastic brethren. But still, all are in competition with one another: televisions and stereos, VCRs and camcorders, computers and microwaves. Component upon component. All with a black check mark along one side. All vying for attention. Short-circuiting and re-routing, forming secret conglomerations, and weeding out the weaklings. Everything molded. Mounted. Mutated. Sending out extension cords and fiber optic cables like sticky tendrils. Bare wires glowing white hot, snapping and hissing. Electricity arcing. Infinite yards of tape reeling out in snares and nets. Cassette tapes, floppy diskettes and CDs sailing through the air at the speed of sound, exploding against their targets. Portals opening wide only to consume anyone who gets to close.

The two never gets too near, of course— keeping to the trail winding down the mountain. Quickly focusing elsewhere. Trying not to draw attention to themselves. For, far too often, even in their short passing, they see many others become trapped and dragged screaming inside. So they ignore the temptations, the promises, the cries of agony, the pleas for mercy. Not now. No. Not ever.

They aren't allowed to pass so easily, however. Although the two are across the valley, they are still detected. Too powerful to be ignored— what an ultimate catch they would make— and they are forced to duck and cover repeatedly. Tapes fly through the air to disable them, disintegrating against the solid rock, showering them with plastic, dust and stony slivers. Meanwhile, brown-black strands of audio and videotape arc through the air, cast out to entangle them. Artificial lightning strikes, shattering the rock face above them. Several times, in electronic suicidal frustration, whole components are launched against them. Surprisingly, there is no avalanche.

Fortunately, their senses are peaked and they are able to make their escape relatively unscathed. Zigging when they have to. Zagging when they need to. There are a few cuts, a few bruises, but nothing is permanently damaged. Separately, retaliation is considered, but neither voices his thoughts. Perhaps another time they will return and set things right. For now, they are relatively safe once again, and that's enough. They only pause long enough to dust themselves off and quickly bind their wounds before they make their way down the mountain.

Farther down the trail, they almost miss a mountain in the distance as there is so little substance to it. Initially, it appears to be only composed of a mass of chaotic black lines, like a giant series of webs, or a jungle gym created by a madman, or simply: a massive modern work of art.

In any case, the two are fascinated and they stop. Focusing their superior sight they see the mountain is formed from words, such as: JUSTICE, FREEDOM, HAPPINESS, SECURITY, and PEACE. Also: POWER, FORTUNE, FAME, and PROPERTY. And: PRIDE, GREED, SELFISHNESS, RIGHTEOUSNESS, RELIGION, and POLITICS. There are many others as well, in a variety of tongues, but all are constructed with the same seemingly fragile spider silk thinness. Words bending, twisting in upon themselves, interlocking, occasionally snapping off and falling away, forgotten; while many meld with others, forming new words entirely.

On the peak's pinnacle, an enormous circular plate wobbles as people move back and forth, round and round— sometimes as individuals, but usually in a variety of groups. As on the other mountain, the people are calling to one another, but here at least there seems to be a more honest attempt at communication. There is still deceit and subterfuge, and elimination, of course. Overall, not a lot of good appears to be accomplished. Often, the balance is lost, and then saved at the last moment, by the proper counter-movement or inspired speech. Nonetheless, these people appear to be getting along a little better here, than on the *homo* mound.

The man clearly remembers his own vision, but he never pictured it on this scale. More than ever, he appreciates the struggle involved— both for the people on their plate and in his own life. Earlier he had some doubts, but now he knows he will do what needs to be done. The weight on his shoulders shifts a bit; although it doesn't leave him, he still feels some measure of relief.

The figure turns to the man. "A result of The Words?"

Nods. "Yes. A match from many millennia ago. The players . . . forgotten, the victor long dead. If they only knew the power of words . . . but every match is unique, of course, so—"

"Still attempting to work everything out?"

The man raises an eyebrow. "Me or them?"

Chuckling. "Answer as you please."

Consideration, then: "Yes . . . Yes . . ."

Then, pointing with his umbrella, the man heads down the trail once more with the figure close behind, still chuckling lightly to himself. The two say no more for quite awhile.

Later in the afternoon, with the heat of the day rising, the swirls above evolve into wisps of bright white. The two come around another curve where they see a volcano steaming, feeding the sky. Basaltic rock rumbles. Trees tremble. Shake. Quake. Eruption is imminent. Yes. Soon. They stand for a short time in silence— closely observing the surrounding geography and each other. Sulphurous fumes and the sickly stench of stewing pork waft over them.

The man puts down his small suitcase and places his umbrella against the rock face. Then he reaches into a pocket. There is a hint of mint in the air.

He holds out the small package. "Gum? Last two pieces."

The figure takes in the offering. "Certainly." And he has a piece. The man unwraps the last one himself and both stand chewing with some satisfaction, enjoying the rest. Both pocket their wrappers.

After a few minutes, the figure turns to the man who is blowing a rather large green bubble.

"How much time do we have?"

The bubble can expand no further and it pops with a soft snap. The man reels in the sagging remnants and starts to chew again.

"That's a rather loaded question, isn't it? Besides, I believe you may know better than I do."

"Indeed." The figure takes off his hat and fans his face for a few moments. Then he wipes his head and the inside of the hat with a blue handkerchief. Replacing both, he carries on: "But I actually only meant to say: how much time before she blows?"

The man pauses. Consideration. Forms a smaller bubble, which he quickly draws back in and sharply snaps it in his mouth.

Then: "We'll be safe."

"Truly?"

Again, the man only nods. "But we should be on our way. Don't worry, we'll be able to see the eruption as we descend. I'm sure it'll be quite the spectacle." He takes up his things and steps past the figure, starting downward through a narrow crevasse.

The figure takes one last look around, then follows, calling after him:

"Have you been up here for very long? Meditating on your mountaintop, perhaps?"

"No. Not long. This was simply my last stop before I returned."

The figure hesitates, finding a handhold. "Well then, who were you talking to just as I arrived?"

Snaps another bubble, then: "The wind."

"The wind?"

"Yes."

"And what did the wind have to say?"

"Nothing." Through the crevasse, the man waits for the figure on a narrow ledge. Sweeps outward with his umbrella. "It was only carrying my words away. Whether or not it hears, understands, or wishes to talk back, I don't know, nor does it particularly matter."

"Do you know where it's carrying your words?"

"Sometimes, but not always. That's partly what makes this so interesting."

"And possibly dangerous."

"Most definitely. Exciting, isn't it?"

"Hmmm? Curious. From what I understand you've certainly changed."

"Have I?" Blows.

The figure decides to let the question go unanswered as the man points to the volcano.

Pops. "Anytime now."

As if on cue, they feel the rock beneath them shake spasmodically, and see the steam blow upward. Eruption occurs. The sky is filled, not with water vapor, volcanic dust and lava bombs, but rather boiling blood, bone dust and human body parts. The sky quickly turns muddy, but fortunately the two are not close enough to be hammered by this onslaught. Not yet, anyway.

The figure lets out a low whistle. "Now *that's* rejection . . . Not a good sign."

The man slowly shakes his head, wondering how much things will change around here, or anywhere else for that matter. For now, he simply opens his umbrella, just in case.

Pops another bubble. "No, but not a surprise either . . . Only a matter of time."

"True enough."

"There's certainly a lot for us to do." And the man turns away from the still erupting volcano and continues his descent. The figure pauses for a moment, taking a last long look before he follows.

"There certainly is."

LIFE IN THE PARKING LANE

Nightfall. Silence in the streets of the obese tabby's domain. The Word has spread. Everyone has cleared the way for their coming. Excited and overwhelmed, but no one wants to be in their way. Wait until the refuse settles, then they'll sneak a peek— see if it's safe. Even if it's not, well, maybe they'll take a chance anyway. They can only miss so much.

The man and the figure walk beside one another— their stride long and even, kicking up garbage along the way. The man bats aside further bits and chunks with the tip of his umbrella, while the figure mentally plays tag with these objects and others— picturing piercing them with his blades.

After a short time they leave their games behind. Their eyes searching. Alert. Expectant. They say nothing, but purposefully make their way down street after street. Their destination: THE SCRATCHING POST.

They round a corner, to see a new sign for the cat's hotel flashing on and off in cool green and violet. An old car battery stands nearby, with lines running up to the sign. The streets remain empty. Only one person, the burly but ragged doorman— tonight in deep forest green— stands at his usual post. Waiting.

Waiting for their approach.

Waiting.

Wait. There is someone else— in the shadows down the street— slowly slithering towards them. The two halt; do some waiting of their own as they see the rather large snake approaching, whom the man recognizes from the obese tabby's memories. The snake stops at a respectable distance while the burly but ragged doorman holds his ground. This has nothing to do with him, of course, but he'll gladly observe and take back whatever he learns to the obese tabby. A bonus is bonus, especially when it comes from the cat.

The snake raises its head high, not quite on the same level as the two men. Its tongue flicks out repeatedly as its body slowly undulates on the asphalt. A short distance away— in the shadows, in the windows and doorways, in the alleys, on the rooftops— vast numbers suddenly appear. Glancing around, the two men notice the Goons and Gronks gathering; more than any they've seen at any other time. All of them armed with their crude weapons, likely, with many more held in secret. None of the Gronks are armored like the obese tabby's pet, but they're not much less intimidating.

They prefer to have as much muscle rippling, vein bursting, steroid pumping, stretch mark tearing, pimple-covered flesh exposed as possible.

Well, so much for no one wanting to be in the two men's way.

The two men hold their ground. Tracking. Counting. Planning: both defense and offense. Now this is a battle worthy of the figure; although he's glad to have the man at his side. Otherwise, even with his phenomenal speed and skill, he likely wouldn't be able to take out the more than five score Goons and Gronks present before some got to him. And more are appearing each moment. The man wonders if this is a trap set by the tabby, even though the cat seemed to have no amiable affiliations with the snake. Besides, an ambush isn't the tabby's style, or so the man has been led to believe.

Meanwhile, the figure has his own idea: the snake is only here for *him.* He never explained to the man what happened to him in The House of Mirrors. The figure wanted to keep that small part of his mythology quiet— to live or die by its own merits, or lack thereof. He hoped the constrictor wouldn't unravel the mystery in order to avoid a scene like this right now, but he knows he didn't cover his tracks very well. Perhaps, deep down, the figure wants someone to question him sometimes. Call him on his actions. Now it appears as though someone is doing just that.

The snake hisses. "Good evening gentlemen."

The man nods as the figure tips his hat. In the background: muscles tense, grips tighten, leather and rubber creak.

"Eventide." The figure calls.

"You know why I'm here, carpenter." It is not a question.

The figure nods while the man looks at him curiously . . . dubiously. *Is he to be betrayed? Is that why The Sentinel was so insistent on him returning here?* The man's pulse quickens, but he decides to hold off for a moment— wait for confirmation. He won't take a life unless it's absolutely necessary. But if the figure has deceived him, he will be the first to perish.

Noticing the man's odd glare, the figure turns to him slightly, suddenly realizing what the man must be thinking. Knowing his life is in considerably greater danger if the man is against him, he speaks carefully. Honestly.

"I know how this may seem, but this has nothing to do with you. I made a mistake earlier and this . . . fine reptile is calling me on it."

During the figure's attempt at an explanation, the man raises his umbrella ever so slightly, pinpointing at least seven different spots where he can direct a quick killing blow against the figure. Then the snake. Then anyone else who chooses to stand against him. He will not tolerate betrayal at all. Ever.

Many notice his gesture, as small as it is, including the figure. However, he makes no attempt to defend himself, not wishing to antagonize the man any further. As soon as the doorman sees the motion, he immediately evaporates, but no one marks his disappearance. He's in the background. His presence is irrelevant— or so many believe— unless there is a door to be opened somewhere.

The figure tries to explain further.

The man raises his umbrella a little more, not yet convinced about this situation, seeing more Goons and Gronks arriving each second. Waiting. Restless. Hungry.

The constrictor draws back— to strike or to flee— that is to be seen.

All around, the Goons and Gronks adjust their positions, moving in, preparing for the inevitable. Slowly stepping forward while even greater numbers take their old positions. Two hundred. Three. Four. More. Catching the fever. Feeling the blood-lust. Wanting vengeance for their fallen brothers. Not wanting explanations. Not wanting to wait any longer. Orders or no orders. Time to move—

Now!

Marking the convergence of the henchmen, the man prepares to thrust while the figure leaves himself exposed, accepting his lot. The doorman suddenly reappears, however, pulling open the door to the hotel, and the obese tabby bursts onto the scene. The Gronks and Goons are caught in mid-motion, instantly aware that there may be a new direction of attack. The man checks his thrust at the last moment, surveying the action, deciding to wait. He may need all his strength yet to take out the henchmen.

The obese tabby bounds towards them as quickly as his heavy body will allow with no concern for his own safety. With a gesture from the cat, the doorman holds his position at the top of the steps. No need to further aggravate the situation just yet. With a flick of the tongue, the snake stops the momentum of his henchmen, if only for a few seconds in order to clarify what exactly is going on here.

Panting profusely, the tabby stops before them, eyeing each in turn. Then he signals to the snake to draw his henchmen back. Grudgingly, the constrictor flicks his tongue again. It takes some time, but the Goons and Gronks eventually pull back; although they're more than prepared to fly forward given the flick. This may not be as easy any longer as the tabby's own henchmen are beginning to arrive in greater and greater numbers. When the Word spreads, it spreads like spilled mercury down a cold steel slide.

Chagrined, the cat begins: "Now gentlemen, this is no way to conduct business, is it?"

The snake hisses, preparing for a rebuttal, but the man speaks first.

"We were on our way to see you, when we were suddenly delayed by this snake and his . . . party." Nods at the figure. "He was attempting to explain things, but confusion grew and the incident escalated rather swiftly. All I seek is clarity. There's no need for all of these—"

"You are correct, of course. Shall we retire to my coffee-shop in private— just the four of us— where we can clear this matter in a much more gentile manner."

"I'd rather not!" The snake snaps.

Hackles rise again. Henchmen lean in all around.

The tabby raises a paw, holding them off a little longer. Frustrated. Annoyed.

"Well, doesn't this bite the green wiener? What exactly would you care to do? Perhaps don't answer that yet— there's too much crossfire to contend with right now."

The man gestures at the figure and the constrictor.

"Perhaps if you two would show us what exactly is between you, then—"

"Ssshow you?" The snake hisses, but the figure understands immediately.

"Yes. Our memories. He has the power to share."

The snake regards the man suspiciously.

"You will not attempt to manipulate our thoughtsss in any way?"

The man shakes his head.

The constrictor considers the idea as well as the man's reputation. He didn't anticipate this situation getting so far out of hand— with the unexpected arrival of the obese tabby and his hundreds of henchmen. He didn't believe the tabby would care one way or the other. Well, so much for his beliefs, and now he can think of no other easier way to end this situation. So, with the odds no longer in his favor, he agrees, if only to slither away from here, alive.

The four come together and the man shares their memories amongst them in regards to The House of Mirrors. The man alters nothing. All four relive the incident involving the misfortune teller and the figure, each in his own way. Afterwards, the discovery of the old woman by the snake is shared in the same manner.

The four eventually come away, each contemplating what he has learned. The man realizes how mistaken he was only moments ago and is ashamed of his suspicions. However, his shame is nothing compared to the figure's regarding the incident in The Mirror House. The snake takes some satisfaction knowing that the figure was able to give the misfortune teller's death some meaning, at least. The tabby feels very little either way. So, he is the first to break their silence. "A sorry event, to be sure. But given the circumstances and his frame of mind under the influence of The House of Mirrors, I'm uncertain if he had any other choice."

Hissing, the snake spits. "I undersssstand why he did what he did, but that ssstill doesssn't make it right. Why ssshould he be allowed to go unpunissshed? Isss he ssso unaccountable for hisss actionsss? What of hisss ressssponsssibilitiesss? I demand jussstticcce."

"Things are different here, as you all know so very well. And there are no courts, no lawmen, only a select number of us each in charge of our own domains."

"Enough! I know you never liked her to begin with and you're glad ssshe'sss been terminated. *I know*. I sssaw your memoriesss, too."

The tongue is flicked.

The henchmen surge forward from all directions— both the snake's and the tabby's in response.

The circle around the four grows smaller. Tighter. Deadlier.

With a sudden gesture from the figure, a shimmering and glimmering portal is created, and he pulls the tabby and the man through behind him, leaving the snake to be swallowed up by his own henchmen. The snake sees the portal disappear before he can reach it, and he sinks to the ground, and attempts to slither away before it's too late.

This time, the perfect disposable henchmen won't be stopped. Goons and Gronks battle one another, the snake's against the obese tabby's, and they even fight amongst their own gangs. Countless scores die, while many are mutilated more than usual, while still others turn and flee into the shadows. The massacre doesn't end for quite a brutal and bloody time.

Whether or not the snake escapes, no one is entirely certain. Many hack and slash at him as he passes underfoot, no longer caring what authority he may or may not have. The next day many claim to have killed the constrictor, holding small chunks of reptilian flesh high in their hands, but no one has the head. More bits of the snake can be found amongst the dead, but then again, there are many other mounds of flesh, bone, and blood, which are also far beyond being recognizable. So, for the time being, the constrictor is considered to be missing in action.

Meanwhile, the figure takes the man and the obese tabby through his portal, and they arrive in one of the private rooms of The Garden of Earthly Delights. It is the same suite in which he and the man recently spent a very short time recuperating just before going to see the obese tabby. Fortunately, the room hasn't been reoccupied yet. Immediately, the figure crosses the suite and pulls twice on the silken cord hanging near the marble mantle, then waits by the door. The man puts his things on the table then takes a seat. Reorienting himself, the cat hops up onto one of the two king size beds in the spacious suite.

A minute later, there is a light knock at the door and the figure opens it only a crack. He whispers a few words to the accommodating madam and she is soon gone. After quietly locking the door, the figure walks over to the table where the man is seated. He takes off his leather bag and his wood lathe, drops them on the carpeted hardwood floor and pulls out a chair. He sits down and throws his booted feet up on the table.

"Personally, I would've liked to have stayed and fought it out. What a glorious battle it could have been! Introducing the snake to my lathe just have done with all this sorry business. But tonight is not about me, and about slaying a thousand Goons and Gronks. Your conflict is too important to be decided in such a brutal and banal manner, regardless of the glory. So I must apologize for not giving either of you any forewarning. In the end I thought it best to escape unscathed . . . What the outcome will be concerning the PR in this matter . . ." The figure pulls out his art. Sees. Shrugs. Sighs. Pockets it. "Well it could go many ways, but it's nothing I can't remedy shortly."

The man holds up his hand. Agitated. "No more. I've heard more than enough."

The cat yawns. "I hope you ordered something from room service when you spoke to the madam. Did you?"

Stewing, the figure remains silent for a moment. He tosses his rumpled hat onto the table, then runs a handkerchief over his bald pate.

"I'm just trying to fulfil my responsibilities as The Sentinel. I understand only too well that things are different here, but still there has to be room to build, to create . . . *myths*. *It's necessary!* Not for me, because it's what I do, or for both of you who are the subjects— or objects, I suppose, as the case may be— but it's for *them*: for the people out there, and even more so, for those in the future. To look back on your legendary adventures and say—"

There's a light knock at the door.

Irritated, the figure storms across the suite, snaps the lock, and rips open the door. Startled, but quickly composing herself, the matronly madam wheels in a cart laden with many of the fine delicacies of her brothel, including: catnip and licorice milk shakes for the tabby, and a pitcher of ice cold spring water for the two men. All three nod their thanks and she softly smiles at them as she swiftly backs out, leaving them to their business.

Regaining his composure, the figure closes the door more gently this time, then relocks the door. The figure pours out two glasses of ice water, and takes these as well as a bowl of freshly roasted pistachios— fortunately without the red dye— over to the table. He returns to the trolley and puts one milk shake and the bowl of herbs on a small tray and places it on the bed before the obese tabby. He takes his seat, has a swallow of water, and then grabs a handful of nuts. Deftly snapping the shells off between two fingers, the figure tosses the nutmeat into his mouth and the shells onto the table, slowly forming a small pile. The man has a few pistachios himself while the tabby gratefully has a pawful of herbs, then begins to slurp his milk shake.

They continue to snack for a short time, with the men relaxing some-what, while the cat's eyes begin to glaze over.

Purring contentedly, he says: "Ahhhh! As much as I am enjoying this, perhaps we should get down to business, gentlemen. To be sure, there's go-ing to be quite the clean-up in the morning, but much more importantly, there is the considerably larger issue between the two of us." He nods at the man, then has another pawful of catnip. Afterwards, the tabby somewhat nervously clears his throat. "Well, what do you propose? A return to The Fray, with an even greater Prize, perhaps?"

The man shakes his head.

Curious but nervous, the cat trembles. "What then?"

The man hesitates, then: "If we are to truly settle things between us, it must be The Words."

Shakes. Quakes. " . . . The Words?"

"Yes."

The tabby takes up a very large pawful of catnip. What he doesn't spill on the bed, he quickly munches and almost chokes. After coughing up a bit, the two men sit up watchfully, but he waves them down and tries to calm himself.

"Although I agree that it is much more dignified; in the past The Words were no less public, and they were monumental in their scope— much more so than The Fray has ever been."

The figure leans back in his chair. "Indeed. The Words have far less flash. Much more substance—"

"And let's not forget the consequences?"

"Of course not."

" . . . I must be honest with you gentlemen, despite my offer after The Fray, I wasn't expecting this at all."

The figure shrugs and continues to crack open pistachios, while the man simply waits for the obese tabby to get it all out.

"What of the stakes? No simple Prize then, I imagine. Our respective realms?"

The man nods. "And more. Much more."

"Ah, but of course."

"It is the way of The Words."

"Indeed."

The tabby pushes away the tray. "When would you like the event to take place?"

The figure leans in. "Do you have everything regarding your realm in order?"

The tabby considers this, then, licking his fangs:

"Yes. I wasn't expecting this, but I was expecting *something*. So: yes. We can begin whenever you like as soon as we can arrange a location and the necessary implements."

Cracks a pistachio. "Excellent."

"Where?"

"In The Coliseum— you two will need the room eventually, I'm sure."

"Fine. I'll make the arrangements immediately . . . with your approval, of course."

The man nods again.

"Well then, gentlemen, if you wouldn't mind giving me a little time to myself to get things in order . . . I'll be with you shortly. Your rooms are available at THE SCRATCHING POST if you still desire them, or you can remain here, of course— the choice is yours."

Then the obese tabby somewhat groggily stands and makes his way for the door. He pauses a moment before leaving, turning to the man.

"Truth be told, as much as I have enjoyed finally meeting you, my Nemesis, I think I enjoyed my previous life a great deal more. It was simpler, more joyful perhaps . . . certainly with a lot less conflict . . . too often mundane, to be sure, but even the mundane has its own charms, its own comforts . . . and I rather liked the mystery of never having actually met you . . ." The tabby drops his head. "Ahhhh, but enough of my whining. We must do what is necessary. So, if you gentlemen will excuse me, I have a lot of preparations to make."

With that, the obese tabby is gone, leaving the two men to their own thoughts— to their own lives before they came here, and they must admit that the cat is right in many ways.

SICK AROUND FOR JOY

Evening. Balancing. Thinking things through. Considering every ehwhatnot. As always.

Time ticks by.

Nothing changes.

Nothing changes.

The man sits. Leaning back. Eyes closed. Alone in The Presidential Suite of THE SCRATCHING POST. The spacious suite's only illumination: several silver candelabras spaced throughout. Their soft, lemony light flickers across his eyelids and he enjoys attempting to follow the motions. Gives him something else to focus on. Distract. Relax. Something. He's thought enough of The Words, but still tomorrow's match with the obese tabby keeps crashing forward in his mind. Won't let him go. Not surprising when so much is at stake. Nonetheless, he would like some peace. Tranquillity. Clear himself of all of his mental baggage and go into the match refreshingly empty. But that remains to be seen. Perhaps he shouldn't try so hard. Perhaps—

There's a knock at the door on the other side of the massive suite. The man keeps his eyes closed listening. Sniffing and tasting the air . . . *Can it be?* Opening his eyes, breathing deeply, he eases out of his seat and strides across the room. It would seem so.

He opens the door in the darkness. A voice calls:

"Hey."

It is he: the prophet stands before him, just as dirty and disheveled as he remembers leaving him in the desert. But there's a new light in his eyes, clarity, lucidity, and something even more familiar: a sharper reflection of himself. *How?* He doesn't know. Nor will he question it now. Instead, the man simply smiles broadly and opens his arms in welcoming. The prophet regards him for a moment, then steps forward and the two hug warmly.

"Come in. Come in."

The prophet steps past and the man closes the door.

"Please, have a seat if you like. Would you care for anything?"

Taking off his satchel and his jacket, the prophet tosses them on the bed then lays down on his back beside them.

Exhaling. "Water . . . just water."

The man pours out two glasses from a crystal pitcher and takes them to the bed. He sits on the edge and passes one to the prophet, who takes the glass in both hands and rests it on his chest for a minute. Lying there, he holds the glass out to the man, but the man is uncertain about the gesture. Then smirking, he leans in and clinks his glass against the prophet's.

"Here's to never seeing another desert again."

The prophet nods his agreement and both take small sips. Begin to relax. Somewhat, anyway.

"I'm glad you made it."

"Ditto."

They sip again, but the two fall into an uncomfortable silence— neither wanting to ask all the usual questions, even though that's really all they can think about. Until finally, the prophet mutters:

"I can't find her."

The man considers this, clearly realizing that he is referring to the young woman.

"I haven't seen or heard about her either since my return. I've only recently arrived, however, and there are many places she could be."

"No. I've been looking for her since my arrival at The Carnival. Some say she was last seen with some Goons— perhaps a week ago or even longer. No one seems to really know. Or at least no one will admit to knowing anything more. But if she was taken away by a gang of Goons, then who knows what's become of her? You can't really tell them apart, so you don't know whom they're working for . . . I have no ideas anyway."

"Would you like me to ask the obese tabby?"

"You can, I suppose . . . But I doubt he'll be any more helpful than the others. I'm concerned . . . but well, mostly I just wanted to let her know I'm leaving again, and I probably won't be coming back. At least, not that I know about."

Sips. "Another test?"

"No. I'm going to try to find my way home again. Maybe if I don't zag when I should really zig, then perhaps I'll find my way and get there in one piece . . . Just so you know, I didn't put in the full forty days and nights, but I had enough of everything and I felt ready to leave— even though I still don't know who or what I returning to or for."

"You'll find out, I'm sure. Besides, sometimes there are more important things. Sometimes, it's the journey that counts the most, moment to moment, not the ending; the supposed climax; or the summation of everything."

"True enough." The prophet finishes his water and puts his glass on a nearby nightstand. The man regards him for a moment.

"I . . . I have something for you."

The man gets up and crosses the room over to his suitcase laying flat on a dresser. Putting down his glass, he pops the latches and opens it. He takes up The Prize in both hands and turns to face the prophet. Sitting up, the prophet watches closely as the man returns to him. The man takes a breath.

"I was going to give this to you when we first met in the desert, but I didn't think you would accept it, seeing it as just another temptation . . ."

The prophet simply nods.

" . . . and in any case, I was uncertain if you really needed it. I thought perhaps you may already possess the knowledge and the power that is contained here." The man softly caresses the etched and embroidered cover. "And even now, I don't doubt your abilities. For whatever reason, whether through an action of yours, someone else's, or whatever the case may be, you have forgotten yourself. And I believe that with this, you'll find yourself again, and you'll find your way home."

The man remains standing a short distance away from the bed, until the prophet comes before him. Holding the book out with both hands, the man utters a short and almost incomprehensible prayer, which, somewhat surprisingly, the prophet finishes with him. Then, he too grasps the book with both hands. There are no massive fireworks, or climactic overtures— only a surge of energy and a flash of insight pass between them. After letting go of the book, the man takes a step back and releases a very heartfelt sigh. The prophet shifts his gaze back and forth between The Prize and the man, excited but uncertain, curious but fearful. Humble.

Turning The Prize over in his hands, the prophet utters:

"The seal hasn't even been broken yet. Haven't you seen for yourself what's contained here?"

"No. At this point in time, I don't wish to possess that knowledge and power. But I'm not simply giving it to you because of that. You *need* it, therefore it is yours."

"But couldn't you use this to help to defeat the obese tabby in The Words?"

"I'm sure The Prize could be used in such a way. But it's not merely a win-lose situation we are dealing with. It's no easy game. There are a great number of levels to its complexity and the consequences are far-reaching. In each their own ways both The Words and The Prize encompass so much more than what meets the eye. For me, the possible advantage of The Prize is both unwanted and unfair. But also, it is potentially very dangerous. Too dangerous perhaps, given the circumstances."

"But wouldn't the obese tabby use it, if he had the opportunity?"

"I'm sure he would, which is another reason why I won't do it, and why

I've now given it to you . . . So please, accept it, but remember to use it wisely."

The prophet gently caresses the seal. "Should I open it now?"

"No. Wait until you are away from here, from this realm. Alone. It won't take you very long. Then, when you are rested, unhurried, crack the seal. But be prepared, it will help you, but sometimes too much knowledge is a deadly friend . . . So take good care of it, and yourself. Once you remember, I'm sure you'll be fine."

The prophet turns away and, reaching across the bed, he pulls over his canvas shoulder bag. Undoing the straps, he pulls out his soiled T-shirt and wraps The Prize in it, then places the package back in his satchel. Suddenly inspired, he reaches for his jacket and pulls out his craft. Turning back to the man, he holds it out in his open palms. The man's eyes widen and he lets out a low, appreciative whistle.

The prophet clears his throat. Takes a breath.

"Since you're giving me something, perhaps I can offer you something in return." He holds it up a little higher, so the man can have a better look at it, then take it for himself. "I made it myself from the remains of my misfortune . . . in the desert, just before I returned here. I don't understand what it does entirely yet, but I do know it's powerful. And I know for a fact it's good for scaring away demons, so that's something useful already."

The man remains where he is and doesn't take his craft away from him. The prophet is both a little hurt and confused, but the man explains:

"Thank you very much, but I can't accept your offer. Just as The Prize is yours, so is your craft. It's very much a part of you— I see that quite clearly— and even though you don't know it well yet, you will someday . . . perhaps someday soon. You need it, just as I need my works."

To emphasize this, the man gently pulls on the chain and draws out his works. Again, there is a surge of energy and awareness between them, and then the moment is gone. The two remain close together, regarding each other warmly, in greater understanding, until the man speaks.

"You see, although I don't understand how or why, you and I and another man are all connected."

"The carpenter?"

"Yes. We are each our own individual self in our own individual times: I am. You are. He is. Perhaps more—"

"But no less."

The man nods. "I have come to believe that in some paradoxical way we are all the same man . . . but again, *different*. I can't explain it and I don't question it. Nor does it concern me greatly. All is as it is." Holds up his works. "But whatever the case, in a similar way, my works, your craft, and his art, are all connected as well. But *now* is not the time for us to come together. Or perhaps we may never come together in any special way. I've had dreams, visions perhaps, but I can't say for certain. The future is not etched in stone . . . So please, keep your craft. Learn from it. Take care of it and it will take care of you."

After briefly caressing his works with his thumb, the man pockets it. Continuing to hold his craft in his hands, the prophet feels both the surface and its depth. Seeking. Searching. Soon finding . . . *a spark*. A quick flash of awakening, of awareness, but then it's gone. Initially, the prophet is upset, desperate, but calms himself, realizing that this is only the beginning. With a blossom of love and respect, he carefully pockets his craft, looking forward to their future together.

"I should be on my way then." And the prophet turns to reach for his leather jacket.

"You don't wish to rest for awhile? Bathe? Shave? Eat? Stick around for The Words?"

The prophet puts on his jacket, then refastens the straps on his satchel.

Drops the strap over his shoulder. "No. Thank you very much, but no. I've made it this far on very little, so I figure I should be able to make it through until the end in the same manner. A kind of penance, perhaps. And as to The Words . . . to tell you a secret, I already know the outcome— I've seen it many times in different ways. You want to talk about having visions— I've had a thousand of them." Taps his skull, somewhat sadly. "Not that I usually understand all of them, mind you, buy . . . Anyway, there's no need for me to stay. My presence would serve little purpose. You'll do what you need to, as always. And then—"

"And then we shall see?"

"Exactly."

The prophet steps away from the man and crosses over to the balcony, where the curtains are drawn back and the glass doors remain closed. The man follows a short distance behind, then comes up beside him. After gazing out onto the street, at the buildings, into the sky, the prophet eventually speaks. His voice is low and even.

"They're waiting . . . For you? Perhaps. For some kind of deliverance? I believe so. Always looking for something better, anyway. What are they doing about it? Not a whole lot . . . they never do . . . just sitting and waiting in their complacency . . . Waiting." Turns to the man. "I'm not sure I can take back what I said to you in the desert— I still can't recommend being a messiah to you, if that's what you're to be. . . I can't give all of my visions away just yet."

"In any case, I have to survive The Words first."

"Yes you do . . . You do."

The prophet reaches out to the man and, for the second time this night, they hug warmly. Then, the prophet turns to go.

"I hope to see you again. I really do."

And he is gone— leaving the man, silent, in the shadows.

QUEEN BEE SYNDROME

Noon. Not your average lunch-time. No. Not today. Today's a different story; a different kind of snack to tide them over. A new myth to unfold. Come alive. Grow.

The Word has spread. The people have gathered, and the Goons, the Gronks, the animals and the vegetables. The minerals? Not bloody likely. They know better and they've high-tailed it for the hills. Well, except for those who are actually taking part in The Words, but that is their lot, fortunately, unfortunately, or misfortunately as the case may be; so they're not to be judged. But, as for all the others: any and all available that wish to cast their own lot are more than welcome. That is, if they are willing to squeeze just a little more forward. A little more together. Just a little tighter and—

Most don't understand what they are casting their lots for— they don't realize the potentially monolithic consequences. They only see the profit, or the possible loss, which they believe they can simply regain another time. Perhaps. Only a few of the elderly, and the even fewer chronically unemployed historians, have any idea what they're in for today— and possibly for endless days to come.

The throngs stand outside The Coliseum like automatons, much worse than sheep. Kept in rows, lined up and waiting: to be entertained. Mesmerized. No concern for any kind of real happening-- only a desire to be dazzled. Posters plastered everywhere. Everyone crying out, affirming:

> "YOU'VE SEEN *THE FRAY* . . .
> NOW EXPERIENCE *THE WORDS!*"

Right. They've been waiting for days— ever since the man's return and the massacre outside THE SCRATCHING POST. Fortunately, no one is holding any grudges over that incident except, possibly, for the rather large snake, but he still can't be found— so it doesn't matter for the moment. Rather, everyone has been focusing on this day, for the ultimate match between the man and the obese tabby. No pets. No henchmen. No sentient mechanisms. Absolutely no substitutes.

The throngs throb. Squeeze. Squabble. Sweat. Sing. Snack on whatever minute, over-priced bits and pieces they can afford, including a few more of the old favorites, like: roasted Styrofoam packing peanuts, honey roasted are extra, candy-coated shoelaces in a rainbow of flavors and colors, and battered and deep-fried nuts n bolts, extra crunchy, of course. Plus, there's the latest sensation sweeping across the realms:

"BOTTLED CHAINS! Get your BARBED BOTTLED CHAINS!"

"Hey, would like a bottle?" One friend asks another. "I hear it's just *deadly*."

"Wish I could, but I only have enough for a yellow snow cone."

"Aww, I'm a bit short, too. Next time . . . Next time . . ."

Anticipation and agitation builds in equal amounts as everyone waits for the doors to be finally open and for The Words to begin. They all have their preferences, but the odds are even either way. Despite what everyone has already seen and heard about the man, the obese tabby has been around here running things for a very long time, and he is not to be underestimated. Whatever gentility and hospitality he displays, the mass knows only too well the cunning, wisdom, and brutality that lie underneath. He's not a mafia kingpin for nothing.

Perhaps more importantly, however, no one here has ever even seen The Words live, and no one knows exactly how it is played. To be sure, they all have their own ideas, which they all believe in with equal exuberance, but no one knows for certain; including the practically extinct historians. All they do know is that, if it involves the man and the obese tabby, it has to be *THE ULTIMATE GAME*— even though no one has played it in nearly countless decades.

All around the people chatter. Almost ceaselessly.

From one: "Are you *sure* it's really The Words. I think that's gotta be a typo and it's really The Swords. Cuz what can you do with words, huh?"

To another: "This better not be just some shouting match. I paid big bone for my ticket. I want to see some blood, at least. Or they'd better show some pretty hot T and A on the side in between rounds, or however this game is played."

And another: "Do you know if they will have the confessions, I mean 'concessions' running? I ran out of food two days ago and I really don't like what they're serving out here."

And another: "When are they going to let *me* in? That's what *I* want to know."

And so on.

Until finally— more felt than heard on the other side of the doors— locks are released and the doors burst open. For a brief moment, there is silence and stillness. Then there is a massive surge forward, an interwoven wave of spectators thrusting into the narrow avenues leading to their assigned seats. Thousands upon thousands cheer and jeer, clap and slap, chomp and stomp but, once again, the first have to wait awhile for everyone to take his or her place.

Packed far beyond capacity with thousands more crowding outside The Coliseum, the masses cry out for their champions. Beneath their feet, beneath their seats and in the aisles, the stones creak and crumble under the overwhelming weight of so many. But no one cares. Even with the stones cracking and falling around them, they're not going anywhere else until they see some action and in the end: *victory*.

Before them on The Coliseum's floor, the implements of The Words stand ready. Waiting. Two gray marble podiums with wisps and swirls of black and white, stand opposite each other fifty feet apart. One podium also has a large cushioned seat before it. Halfway between the podiums, but to one side, a massive golden barrel is supported on its side. On one end, there is a two-handed crank, and the entire surface of the barrel is covered with deeply carved but seemingly incomprehensible markings. In the middle of the barrel, facing the center, there is a chute ending in a covered reservoir, with a second reservoir on a short stand nearby.

This set-up causes further deliberation and confusion. The crowds become rowdier each minute, with most lines beginning with:

"Now let me tell you what *I* think . . ."

Or: "Let me tell you what *I* want to see happen . . ."

Over the din, a voice cries out: "This had better not be some BINGO tournament!"

There is a wave of laughter, and further calls and cries. Many become upset, believing they may have spent whatever little wealth they have just to witness some glorified number calling.

Not wishing to wait any longer, the crow takes wing from his perch in his private booth, and starts to soar and swoop over the crowds. He takes stock— noting likely rabble-rousers, the positions of his protective Goons and Gronks, and the best escape routes. There are considerably fewer henchmen than usual for such an event, which the crow is not at all happy about, but they're not his to dispatch. In any case, after the recent fiasco, there's not much that can be done until new batches can be prepared. But that will take quite some time. Genetic engineering can only go so quickly these days.

Below the crow, the throngs are whipped into an even greater maniacal frenzy, knowing his presence marks the beginning. The tremors can be felt throughout The Carnival and even in several nearby realms. As the crow finally takes his position high above The Coliseum's floor, the people begin to clap and chant:

"WORDS! WORDS!! WORDS!!! WORDS!!!! WORDS!! WORDS!!! WORDS!!!! WORDS!!!!! WORDS!!! WORDS!!!! WORDS!!!! WORDS!!!!!!"

A horn blares five quick notes.

The crowds roar: "WOOOOOOOOOORRRRRDDSSSSS!!!!!!!"

The horn.

The crowds.

The horn.

The crow.

And the crowds are silenced.

He squawks, his voice surprisingly subdued: "Good afternoon my distinguished ladies and gentlemen. Welcome to this day's Words."

"WOOOOOOOOOOOOOOOOOOOOOORRRRRRRRRRDDDSSSSSS!!!!!!"

"Yes. Today's very special fray as you know all so well is between the obese tabby and his Nemesis—"

"FRAY!! FRAY!!! FRAY!!!! FRAY!!!!! FRAY!!! FRAY!!!! FRAY!!!!! FRAY!!!!!!"

Batting his wings. "Yes. Yes. Yes. But before they come out here and begin, I would like to go over a few ground rules, and tell you what The Words entail."

"SHADES OF GRAY!!!! SHADES OF GRAY!!!!!!!! SHADES OF GRAY!!!!!!!!!! SHADES OF GRAY!!!!!!!!!!!!!!!!"

Raising his voice: "It would be gre—"

"SSHHHHHAAAAAAAAAADDESSSSS!!!!!!!!!!"

"—ciated if you could kee—"

"OFFFFFFFFF!!!!!!!!!!"

"—lume down, as The Words req—"

"GRRRRRRRRRRAAAAAAYYYYYYYYYYYYYYYY!!!!!!!!!!"

"—of concentration."

The horn blares its cacophonous cry once more.

"WOOOOOOOOOOOOOOOOOOOOORRRRRRRRRRDDDSSSSS!!!!!!!!!!"

"Oh very well then . . . HERE THEY ARE!!!!!"

The crowds go utterly insane as the crow takes to the air once more and the trio enters the arena: the figure leads the obese tabby and the man, who come out together side by side. The figure is untooled and he has even left his hat at the hotel. His leather is scrubbed and oiled, however, just as the man's suit is freshly pressed, and the tabby's short hair is thoroughly brushed. Other than his clothing, the man has left his works behind, as well as all his possessions. The cat is unadorned, just as he was made. As always.

The trio crosses over The Coliseum's floor and each takes up his position. The figure stands by the handle of the great golden drum, while the man and the obese tabby stand before it at opposite ends. They face each other. Fortunately, all three have phenomenal hearing and are able to pick out the crow's words above the unceasing thunder of the masses.

The crow flaps his wings, loosely hovering before them.

"Gentlemen. I'll be brief, as no one is listening except the three of you, but you're all that matter, anyway. You know the rules and how important this match is for all of us. I only hope you'll be able to concentrate and focus your energy amongst all this fanfare. So, play well and play honestly, and listen for my judgement calls. I'll be watching very closely . . . Good fortune to both of you . . . Now if you'll excuse me, gentlemen . . ." The crow soars high above. Then: "LET THE WORDS BEGIN!!!!!"

Once again, the crowds chant and stomp while the stones of The Coliseum crumble beneath them. They watch with intense interest as the figure turns the handle of the barrel with both hands.

A low rumbling emanates from inside the drum. As the air passes over the spinning surface of the slowly accelerating barrel, there is also the sound of breathing, as if the barrel is coming to life. The masses are drawn into an uneasy silence as the drum spins faster and the thunder increases inside of it: wildly galloping, then stampeding like a massive herd of buffalo, crushing everything in its path. The breathing deepens, but there are also sudden odd catches and coughs, whines and wheezes, and the throngs stir uncomfortably.

Eventually the figure opens the chute, and several dozen brightly glowing, colored stones roll and bounce downward into the covered reservoir. He stops cranking the handle and gently applies a hand brake. The barrel shrieks— seemingly in agony— and sparks fly, while the masses gasp and cry out. Most tremble in fear. Many stand weeping. Already, a small number have started to leave, shoving their way out. They simply can't witness this event, whatever the outcome.

The crow calls from his perch high above: "Whoever draws an *A* or the letter closest to it may draw his twelve letters first and begin The Words!"

There are a number of cheers but most remain silent for the moment. Watching. Waiting.

The man steps forward, gesturing. "After you."

"Pshawh. You are my guest, and in this event, you are the visiting team, so to speak, so please—"

The man nods and draws a ruby letter from the reservoir. The tabby draws an emerald of his own and, at the same time, the two hold them up for the crow to see. The man holds a *C*, while the tabby holds an *M*.

"Well then," the crow squawks, gesturing with his wings at the man, "you are to have the first draw and begin The Words."

This time, the crowds cheer more enthusiastically, trying to forget their fears. There is also a small smattering of boos from those who bet on the first draw and lost. Overall, despite the eerie drum, most are simply happy that The Words are finally under way. The figure uncovers the reservoir, and the opponents drop their stones in it. Then tracing his fingers over the surface, he finds the small lid of the barrel, opens it, and pours the stones back inside. The two stand aside as the figure turns the handle once more. Again, the thunder of 365 stones rolls inside this living, breathing barrel. The masses are quieted.

Soon satisfied that the stones are thoroughly mixed, the figure re-opens the chute. After twelve stones have tumbled down, the man takes the covered reservoir to his podium. Then the figure repeats the process for the obese tabby, who takes the reservoir to his seat before his podium. Finished, the figure releases the handle and applies the hand brake more firmly this time. The barrel squeals and shrieks again, and sparks spray higher in the air, scaring away even more people. It continues to wail until it finally revolves to a stop. There are wisps of burnt metal in the air, not much unlike the smell of burnt flesh. Undisturbed, the figure steps back and keenly observes all.

The masses shuffle and scuffle as they wait for the man to make his first move. Most still don't know what to expect, and they find the relative inactivity somehow both exhilarating and annoying.

Then, without any warning, the man gathers up a handful of stones and throws them out directly at the obese tabby. There is a massive intake of breath all around as the stones fly through the air, but then stop short exactly in the middle, and hover in midair, rearranging themselves.

"AAAAAAWWWWWWWWWWWWWWWWWWWWWWW!!!!!!!"

The audience trembles and sighs, surprised and disappointed that the stones didn't go all the way to the cat. Growing to the size of melons, the stones begin to glow, and the people become momentarily fascinated with this minor display. Despite the relatively small size of the letters, everyone throughout The Coliseum can easily read the word— well, those few who know how to read, that is— as it floats in the air:

TRUSTING

The figure nods in understanding while the tabby rearranges his letters on his podium. Compensating. Considering. All around, the people look to one another for some kind of insight, but come up with nothing. Before anyone can say anything, however, the cat casts his own stones, which sail through the air, expanding in mid-flight. One lands above the *U*, and the others form directly below it, creating the word:

QUARREL

Somewhat saddened, the man sighs, and all three converge on the barrel once again to build their letters back up to twelve. All three remain quiet.

Above and around, many cheer, some in a minute sense of understanding. For most, however, they are simply glad to see there is some flash and a confrontation arising. Many even start to bicker amongst themselves, debating the meaning of the words spelled, and where this fray is going.

The barrel rolls once more, but as everyone knows what to expect, they're not half as disturbed as they were only minutes before. Many lean forward in expectation. Others slowly begin to chant and stomp, but the wave is not riding high again, yet.

Restocked, the man and the obese tabby return to their podiums and begin to move their letters around. On his podium, the man spells B_TTLE, for BATTLE, but angered and not wanting to go that route, he substitutes the Ts for Bs and casts his stones. The letters fly, then form around the *A* in QUARREL, and perpendicular to TRUSTING to spell:

BABBLE

There is a host of boos and catcalls while the chanting slowly rises a few decibels. Seeing the power of his quarrel reduced, the obese tabby grins, unfazed. With a hint of mischief in his eyes, he plays with his letters for a few moments longer. Lingering. Snickering, he gathers his stones and tosses them to the center to spell:

SURPRISE

Crossing over the second *R* in QUARREL, his new word runs parallel to TRUSTING. The man is drawn deep into his thoughts, wondering what the tabby has in mind— a surprise being no less aggressive, but potentially, even more devastating than a quarrel; especially in this case, where the surprise is based on the quarrel.

For the third time, the drum rolls. As there are fewer stones inside, the thunder changes pitch and tone, and the breathing becomes slightly more wheezy and whiny: none of which is any less unsettling for the spectators above.

Back at their podiums, the man wastes no time and throws out a handful of stones, hoping to counter the tabby's surprise. The stones create a crescent crossing over at the *U* and at the second *R* in SURPRISE to form the word:

LAUGHTER

No one is laughing, however. There is a heavy resonance of booing all around, and many start to throw their own bits of stones, garbage, or whatever else is handy. Most wonder why the obese tabby has said nothing. The common cry is:

"THAT'S NOT FAIR!!!! HE CAN'T DO THAT!!!!"

The crow swoops down, flapping his wings, trying to calm the audience.

"If you'll let me explain . . ." And the crow has to duck in order to evade a large chunk of masonry. " . . . His double-block and redirection are entirely within the boundaries of the rules."

"You never told us that!" A heckler cries and throws a broken bottle.

"You never gave me the oppor—" swoops, then nods at a gang of Goons to take the rabble-rouser away. "Oh, never mind! Ladies and gentlemen, you must contain yourselves—"

"WORDS! WORDS!! WORDS!!! WORDS!!!!"

"Very well then." The crow takes flight, and the heckler is beaten and dragged away to be taken care of properly.

As soon as the crow has cleared away, the obese tabby casts his stones, forming his own crescent— from the *L* on QUARREL to the second *S* on SURPRISE. The word being:

LESSON

The throngs roar— not so much for the word, as for the tabby forming a crescent of his own: what's good for the man is good for the cat.

The man considers the growing puzzle before him as he receives his replacement letters. The letters in the center are triple the size they were in the first round, and now with the crescents, The Words have become both twisted and complicated. Indeed. In deed.

At his podium, the man sighs in some relief as he sees a possible solution before him. He throws, creating a diagonal, crossing the *N* on LESSON and adding a *D* to SURPRISE. The word:

AMEND

Flinching at the huge set-back, the feline desperately rearranges his letters.

From above there is a rain of boos and a hail of refuse. None attempt to protect themselves, as there is nothing too threatening. Besides, they have much more important matters before them than their own personal safety. Instinctively, however, the Goons and Gronks close their protective circle a little more tightly around the trio.

All around people call out:

"Is he kidding . . . this must be some kind of joke!"

"Where did he learn to play? *I* could play better than him."

"I am severely, severely bored! Pass me a peanut."

"I put in my lot for this? I'm outta here."

Others, wanting to forget The Words, start to chant:

"FRAY! FRAY!! FRAY!!! FRAY!!!! FRAY!! FRAY!!! FRAY!!!! FRAY!!!!! FRAY!!! FRAY!!!! FRAY!!!!! FRAY!!!!!!"

Ignoring all of this, the obese tabby almost chooses to spell SCRIBE. He changes his mind at the last moment, however, not certain if he can later support such a tangent. So instead, he reforms his letters, then tosses his stones, running his word parallel to BABBLE, and ending on the *E* in LESSON:

BRIBE

The crowds erupt at this apparent betrayal and let their own stones fly. The chips of stone, people's shoes, remnants of their snacks, and anything else they can get their hands on pelt all three on the arena floor. Covered in grime and small cuts and bruises, the three move quickly to begin the next round. The circle around them grows smaller, and these henchmen receive their own fair share of flying debris. After the two have their new letters, the figure continues to slowly turn the handle in order to speed things up for the next round.

It is no surprise when the man casts his stones forming his word across the *I* in BRIBE:

AGAINST

The tabby persists, however, spelling downward from the first *S* on SURPRISE:

SELLING

The Words continue to grow and glow, filled with the power of their meaning and their complex interaction. As well, they're reacting to the masses around them, which is becoming more frenzied every minute.

In the next round, the man spells downward across the *T* on AGAINST:

POVERTY

Then the tabby quickly spins a hairpin around the *O* and ending on the *Y* in POVERTY.

ACTSOFJOY

The crowds go furiously insane.

"That's more than one word!"

"What kind of mafia kingpin does that obese tabby think he is?"

"That man is supposed to be our savior? *I* could be a better messiah."

"Pass me another peanut— then I think I'm outta here, too."

The two already move on to the next round.

Spelling downward across the *H* on LAUGHTER, the man attempts to take care of things in the way of The Words:

LIGHTSOUTMEN

Many fall unconscious while others fall to their deaths. Still others run shrieking away from The Coliseum as best they can. Most don't make it, however, being swallowed up by the remaining angry mobs around them.

The obese tabby goes on a bit of tangent this time by spelling his word across the *E* in LIGHTSOUTMEN:

CREATIVE

This time, having nothing else in their possession, the people let their misfortune fly at the trio on the floor. Blood seeps from a multitude of wounds on all of them, but still they won't be stopped. Feeling a calm sense of resolution and brotherhood, the man and the obese tabby take their letters back to their podiums, and continue to rearrange the letters. The circle tightens even more, and the henchmen are constantly attempting to block the debris. Many are struck down themselves, but all those remaining proudly stand their ground. High above, the crow observes, largely unscathed, but keeps one eye on an exit at all times now.

Just after they reach their podiums, a blow to the back of his head from a rather large television component strikes down the figure. The two see him fall and watch for a moment, as blood pours from the open wound in his skull. Whether or not he will live they don't know. Immediately, a gang of Goons converges on him and takes him away as quickly as possible, beating their way through the crowds. Seeing as this is likely the last round, the two know they will have to do their absolute best.

Still, the misfortune continues to fly, hammering the two below, despite the valiant efforts of the dwindling number of henchmen. The throngs continue to chant and stomp, and whole sections of The Coliseum start falling apart, taking anyone nearby to their deaths. In the midst of all the destruction, many reach out to be saved. Expecting it. Demanding it. But no one helps anyone else at all. Everyone only looks out for his or her own self, so many more die unnecessarily. Not that there are any necessary deaths to begin with.

With a smile of satisfaction, the man casts his last round of stones, forming his word downward, across the *C* on CREATIVE:

PEACETOMORROW

Without hesitation, the tabby lets his own fly, crossing over the middle *O* on PEACETOMORROW:

DONETRULY

He returns the man's smile, but before they can enjoy their mutual victory, both are struck down. The obese tabby takes a chunk of glass into his right eye, and the man receives several blows on his head and chest.

Neither rises from The Coliseum's floor as the massive structure is demolished all around them. The few remaining henchmen close on the two, and these are hammered more than ever as they try to take their bodies away.

Still, the misfortune flies, until there is nothing left, and nobody left to throw.

THE BLESSING OF TEARS

Nocturne. In the distance, the fringes— a hollow voice resonates lightly, but filled with melancholy.

The obese tabby wakes. Eyelids flutter in the dim lighting of his spacious suite. One lid impeded. He sits up startled. Panicking. Reaches for his eyes. Feels the bandage covering the right. Feels the pain all over again— not that it ever left— but now it's all he can think about. And the loss. So much lost.

He eases his battered body back against his plush pillows, breathing deeply. Trying to calm himself. Trying to remember what happened . . . *When? How long has he been unconscious?* He doesn't know. Despite all his dreams, none have given him any clues as to how long he has been in his bed, or how he got here in the first place. No. His dreams were of a different variety altogether. *Prophetic?* Perhaps. But he would rather not venture in that direction just yet. Especially not after The Words. First he'll need information as to the final results, and what has happened since he's been out of the game. So many questions. If only he had a bowl of his finest to help carry him through until then. If only—

The young woman enters, singing quietly to herself: a porcelain bowl in one hand, and a small tray with bandages, tape, some small towels, and scissors in the other. The tabby's face brightens for a moment until he sees the contents of the bowl: it's only water. Sighing forlornly, the cat sinks even deeper into his pillows and pulls up his goose down duvet.

Seeing the obese tabby awake, she stops singing. The young woman sits beside him on the bed and puts the items on the nightstand. She is no longer filthy, with her hair and skin freshly washed, and she has changed her clothes for the first time in a *very* long time. Gone are her moth-ravaged coat and tattered blouse and jeans, to be replaced by a simple sun dress. She is barefoot. Despite her present cleanliness and lucidity, however, the cat believes her to be no less insane. As well, her wild, varicose eyes carry a certain sadness the cat has never seen before in her. He gazes at her curiously with his one eye, while she carefully begins to remove his bandage.

"How long have I been unconscious?"

She hesitates for a moment. "Three days."

" . . . So long . . .?"

"Don't worry, everything's been taken care of, as well as can be expected, anyway." She nods knowingly. Broadly. "I know my responsibilities. Yes I do. Without a doubt. I take the time—"

"But of course." The tabby swallows. Hard. "And my right eye?"

"Gone. But a collection has been taken up from the remnants of Hubris' Taxidermy store, and you'll have a fine choice of glass ones to choose from . . . after you've healed properly." She tilts her head. Blinks. "Everyone knows their responsibilities now. Yes they do." Nods again. Spittle on her lips.

The bandage removed, the young woman dips one of the towels in warm water and dabs it at his wounded eye socket. The tabby winces, but holds his place as best as he can, knowing she means him no harm. Still, he mews.

"Have you no catnip with you?"

The young woman shakes her head roughly, spittle flying onto his duvet.

"Sorry. I wasn't expecting you to be awake. No sir. But I can get some for you after I am finished here. Yes I can."

"Thank you . . . Thank you."

She places a square bandage against his eye. "Hold this in place for me while I wrap some gauze around."

As the young woman unrolls the gauze, the tabby's thoughts drift until they finally settle upon his Nemesis and The Sentinel.

After she secures the new bandage, he barely manages:

"What of the others?"

Crestfallen, her shoulders slump, and the young woman looks past the tabby: far away and nowhere at the same time. Her hands drop into her lap and she sits there dully for more than a minute. Mouth hanging loosely open. Drool starting to drip. Finally, the obese tabby nudges her a few times until she barely utters:

" . . . Gone."

Alarmed, the tabby springs up, receiving a massive rush a pain racing through his head. He shakes her, but she remains eerily distant. Drip. Drip. Drip.

"*Gone?* What do you mean *gone?*"

In a low monotone she replies: "After you three had all fallen, everyone's misfortune continued to fly."

Drip.

"Then, when they had nothing else to throw, they threw themselves towards you. Rushing the floor. The few Goons and Gronks left gathered all three of you up, then brought you here so you wouldn't be torn apart."

Drip.

"At least, I'd thought they'd all brought you here, but the henchmen that carried the carpenter away first never arrived. They've all disappeared and there's no trace of them to be found. Nowhere. No sir. Not at all."

Drip.

Wondering aloud, the tabby mutters: "The snake's doing?" But she doesn't answer his question, so he asks another, much more important to him: "What of my Nemesis?"

" . . . Dead."

Drip.

The obese tabby's eye widens in disbelief while tears well in the young woman's eyes. The cat chuckles in stops and starts, but there is no humor in his laughter.

"Pshawh. You must be joking. He cannot be dead."

"He was a man." And the tears fall.

"But no average man, to be sure. Where is he?"

"Your henchmen took him directly to his suite three days ago. I cleaned and bound his wounds, but it was already too late. I left him there, uncertain what to do with his body. Then I thought of that bit of metal he always carries and placed it in his hand. It started to click and grind and glow for a little while, but he still just lay there. His wounds healed a bit that day, but then stopped. Nothing more has happened since then, either, at least not that I've seen, but I left it in his hand just in case. I was expecting you to wake sooner, thinking you would know what else to do."

Drip.

Ripping his covers away, the obese tabby flips over to his paws— his head reeling, his heavy body aching.

"Take me to him, *now*."

The young woman looks at him dumbly for a moment, as if finally awakening, then slowly stands. She helps ease him off his bed and, together, they make their way to the double doors of his suite. As quickly as they can, they walk down the hall passing several protective Goons and Gronks along the way. They all nod their approval as the two go by, happy in their own way that the old mafia kingpin is on his feet once more.

The two reach the door to The Presidential Suite and enter it without hesitation. Across the massive room, a figure lies on the bed, covered with a single white sheet. The tabby bounds as swiftly as his wounded, heavy body will carry him and manages to leap up onto the bed. His head and heart hammer furiously but he ignores their warnings. Immediately, he draws back the sheet to see the pale form of his Nemesis lying there naked, face up, with his arms at his sides, and his works resting in his open right palm. His lean body is covered with an elaborate map of scars, both old and new.

Mewing forlornly, the obese tabby checks for any signs of life: for breathing, a pulse, warmth, anything, but finds nothing. He rubs his head against the man's, back and forth, purring hoarsely, tears streaming, wishing him alive.

The young woman steps up behind the obese tabby, and places a comforting hand across his back. Stroking him gently, she whispers, her face wet, glistening in the dim light of the suite:

"I told you truly . . . He has shown no signs of decay, but he has shown no signs of life either."

The cat stops rubbing himself against the man as he considers her words. There is no rotting. No redolence. Feeling the man's face with his paws, the obese tabby also feels a whisper of warmth, but he can't be certain if it's simply his own heat he is feeling. Desperate but uncertain, he considers the possibilities, but arrives at no clear solution.

"I have no idea how to operate his works, or if anyone other than him can even manipulate it. His works may have depleted itself already in that first day on its own . . . I don't know . . .With both The Sentinel and the prophet gone, I can think of no other way to help him, or if he's even still within our reach. I'm no doctor, and there are none to be found anywhere that I'm aware of."

"Are you giving up so easily?"

"We don't know if he would want to be revived, or if that is even possible. Perhaps it would simply be for the best to give him an honorable burial."

"*I can't believe it!* After everything you two have been through—"

Holds up a paw, stopping her. "I don't come by this decision easily." Realization dawns. "But then again, he's really your Nemesis now— *your responsibility.* For, as we agreed— since even before The Words began— what was once mine is now all yours. So you may do with him as you please; although I do hope you'll take my advice . . ." Sighs. "It's unfortunate he'll never know I had given everything to you, and I was only playing with my own very self. I think he would've appreciated the joke."

"Perhaps. He had a very weird sense of humor."

The obese tabby smiles up at her warmly. "Whatever you decide, take excellent care of him— he's a very worthy man." After gently brushing a paw against the man's face, he leaps off of the bed.

"You don't have to go so soon." She drops to her knees. "Really! I'm in no great hurry to—"

The tabby takes her hands in his paws. Locks his eye on both of hers. She is crying again.

"I have forgotten myself, and I have no place here any longer."

"Please take it back. What's yours is yours."

He squeezes, not too gently. "No. A deal is a deal. Besides, I no longer want the responsibility."

"Well, how about as a friend then? He could use one right now. So could I."

"You have each other, so to speak, and I have my own journey to embark on. Staying would only complicate and confuse matters. It would only make things difficult, and possibly far more dangerous. However, I'll check into the results thus far concerning The Words and the respective realms. And I'll make sure the Word spreads concerning your rising."

The obese tabby squeezes her hands again, but in a much more affectionate manner. The young woman returns the pressure, equally warm. She will do what needs to be done.

"Have a safe journey then . . . Good fortune to you."

"And for you as well."

And with that, the obese tabby makes his way for the door, leaving his life as a mafia kingpin behind— leaving it for a much simpler, more mundane, but easier life to live— or so he hopes.

For the time being, anyway.

ERASERHEAD PRESS BOOKS
www.eraserheadpress.com

Eraserhead Press is a collective publishing organization with a mission to create a new genre for "bizarre" literature. A genre that brings together the neo-surrealists, the post-postmodernists, the literary punks, the magical realists, the masters of grotesque fantasy, the bastards of offbeat horror, and all other rebels of the written word. Together, these authors fight to tear down convention, explode from the underground, and create a new era in alternative literature. All the elements that make independent films "cult" films are displayed twice as wildly in this fiction series. Eraserhead Press strives to be your major source for bizarre/cult fiction.

SOME THINGS ARE BETTER LEFT UNPLUGGED
by Vincent W. Sakowski.

A post-modern fantasy filled with anti-heroes and anti-climaxes. An allegorical tale, the story satirizes many of our everyday obsessions, including: the pursuit of wealth and materialism;the thirst for empty spectacles and violence; and climbing whatever social, political, or economical ladder is before us. Join the man and his Nemesis, the obese tabby, and a host of others for a nightmare roller coaster ride from realm to realm, microcosm to microcosm: The Carnival, The Fray, The Garden of Earthly Delights, and The Court of The Crimson Ey'd King. Pretentious gobbledygook or an unparalleled anti-epic of the surreal and absurd? Read on and find out.
ISBN: 0-9713572-2-6, 156 pages, electronic: $4.95, paperback: $9.95

SZMONHFU
by Hertzan Chimera

Fear the machine - it is changing. The change comes not only from the manner of my life but from the manner of my death. I will die four deaths; the death of the flesh; the death of the soul; the death of myth; the death of reason and all of those deaths will contain the seed of resurrection. This is the time of the stomach. This is the time when we expand as a single cell expands. The flesh grows but the psyche does not grow. That is life.

ISBN: 0-9713572-4-2, 284 pages, electronic $4.95, paperback $15.95

THE KAFKA EFFEKT
by D. Harlan Wilson

A collection of forty-four short stories loosely written in the vein of Franz Kafka, with more than a pinch of William S. Burroughs sprinkled on top. A manic depressive has a baby's bottom grafted onto his face; a hermaphrodite impregnates itself and gives birth to twins; a gaggle of professors find themselves trapped in a port-a-john and struggle to liberate their minds from the prison of reason—these are just a few of the precarious situations that the characters herein are forced to confront. The Kafka Effekt is a postmodern scream. Absurd, intelligent, funny and scatological, Wilson turns reality inside out and exposes it as a grotesque, nightmarish machine that is always-already processing the human subject, who struggles to break free from the machine, but who at the same time revels in its subjugation.
ISBN: 0-9713572-1-8, 216 pages, electronic: $4.95, paperback: $13.95

SATAN BURGER
by Carlton Mellick III

A collage of absurd philosophies and dark surrealism, written and directed by Carlton Mellick III, starring a colorful cast of squatter punks on a journey to find their place in a world that doesn't want them anymore. Featuring: a city overrun with peoples from other dimensions, a narrator who sees his body from a third-person perspective, a man whose flesh is dead but his body parts are alive and running amok, an overweight messiah, the personal life of the Grim Reaper, lots of classy sex and violence, and a fast food restaurant owned by the devil himself. 2001, Approx. 236 min., Color, Hi-Fi Stereo, Rated R.
ISBN: 0-9713572-3-4, 236 pages, electronic: $4.95, paperback: $14.95

SHALL WE GATHER AT THE GARDEN?
by Kevin L. Donihe

"It illuminates. It demonizes. It pulls the strings of the puppets controlling the strangest of passion plays within a corporate structure. Everyone, every thing is a target of Mr. Donihe's wit and off-kilter worldview . . . There are shades of Philip K. Dick's wonderfully inventive The Divine Invasion (minus the lurid pop singer), trading up Zen Buddhism for unconscious Gnosticism. Malachi manifests where Elijah would stand revealed; and the Roald Dahl-like midgets hold the pink laser beam shining into our hero's mind. Religion is lambasted under the scrutiny of Corporate money-crunchers, and nothing is what it seems." - From the introduction by Jeffrey A. Stadt
ISBN: 0-9713572-5-0, 244 pages, electronic: $4.95, paperback: $14.95

SKIMMING THE GUMBO NUCLEAR
by M.F. Korn
A grand epic wasteland of surreal pandemic plague. Pollution quotient in the southern delta nether regions of the state of Louisiana, the dustbin of the Mississippi river and the nation, whose motto is the "Sportsman's Paradise" but is a paradise of colorful denizens all grappling for a slice of lassez bon temps roule, "let the good times roll", but now all are grappling for their very lives. Nature had to fight back sooner or later, and now what will happen to this tourist state gone amuck with middle-ages plague?
ISBN: 0-9713572-6-9, 292 pages, electronic: $4.95, paperback: $16.95

STRANGEWOOD TALES
edited by Jack Fisher
This anthology is a cure for bland formulaic horror fiction that plagues supermarkets and drugstores. It shames so-called "cutting-edge" publishers who are really just commercial wannabes in disguise. And opens doors to readers who are sick of writers afraid to break out of the mold and do some-thing/anything different. Featuring twenty insane tales that break all rules, push all boundaries. They can only be described as surreal, experimental, postmodern, absurd, avant-garde or perhaps just plain bizarre. Welcome to the dawning of a new era in dark literature. Its birthplace is called STRANGEWOOD. Featuring work by: Kurt Newton, Jeffrey Thomas, Richard Gavin, Charles Anders, Brady Allen, DF Lewis, Carlton Mellick III, Scott Thomas, GW Thomas, Carol MacAllister, Jeff Vandermeer, Monica J. O'Rourke. Gene Michael Higney, Scott Milder, Andy Miller, Forrest Aguirre, Jack Fisher, Eleanor Terese Lohse, Shane Ryan Staley, and Mark McLaughlin.
ISBN: 0-9713572-0-X, 176 pages, electronic: $4.95, paperback: $10.95

COMING SOON:
"Skin Prayer" by Doug Rice, "My Dream Date (Rape) with Kathy Acker" by Michael Hemmingson, and a reprinting of "Electric Jesus Corpse" by Carlton Mellick III

Order these books online at **www.eraserheadpress.com**
or send cash, check, or money order to 16455 E Fairlynn Dr. Fountain Hills, AZ 85268

LaVergne, TN USA
24 October 2010
202069LV00003B/44/A